To a beautiful &
adventurous couple.
Happy Wedding Day,
  Happy Marriage!

In Christ,
  Mark & Sarah Williamson

P.S. We are going to come
  visit you Someday!

My Heart Lies South

THE STORY OF MY MEXICAN MARRIAGE
YOUNG PEOPLE'S EDITION

MY HEART LIES SOUTH

The Story of My Mexican Marriage

YOUNG PEOPLE'S EDITION

ELIZABETH BORTON DE TREVIÑO

BETHLEHEM BOOKS • IGNATIUS PRESS

BATHGATE, N.D.   SAN FRANCISCO

This special young people's edition has been slightly revised by the publisher to make it more suitable for general family reading.

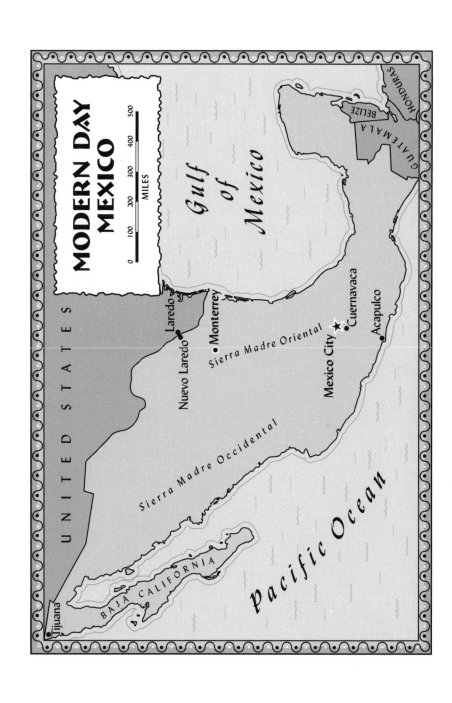

To Mamacita and Papacito
I dedicate this book
in loving memory

I

"MISS BORTON!" bawled my city editor. I hurried up to his desk.

"You're always yammering about going to Mexico," he said. "Here's a bunch of due bills. Airplanes, trains, hotels. . . . Take 'em and see how far you get. When you run out of money, write something for us."

I got as far as San Antonio, and there I called on a man whose name the city editor had given me.

"Look up this man," my editor had said. "He loves every inch of the highway from Laredo to Mexico City. He's always lecturing about it. If you can get as far as San Antonio, he can probably get you the rest of the way."

The name was William Harrison Furlong.

Kindly big Bill Furlong took me under his wing, and personally drove me to Laredo, where, in answer to his insistent wire, the Monterrey Chamber of Commerce had dispatched its young public relations man to receive me, waft me across the border, and conduct me to Monterrey with the dignity due the newspaper I represented.

Accordingly I sat in a hotel lobby in Laredo with Mrs. Furlong and Bill when the emissary from Monterrey arrived. It was very hot and the young Mexican who hurried into the lobby mopping his brow, only one hour late, was

1

dressed in a short-coated white linen suit and carried a *jipi-japa*, which is the south-of-the-border version of the boater.

This was my first glimpse of my husband.

Tall and spare, with large sad black eyes, black curly hair, a fine beak of a nose, a small Spanish mouth outlined by a sparse black mustache, he is, he says, "the villain type." He was tired and hot and he looked at the lady who was to be his charge with scant interest, politely bowing.

"Hello Luis!" said Bill. "This is Miss Borton. When you get to Vallecillo, buy her an ice-cold beer."

Luis laughed nervously. There is nothing he likes better than a cold beer, but the lady he had taken across the border for the Chamber of Commerce two weeks before had resisted the beer with desperation as if it might be the first step in a seduction, and the lady last week had been Dorothy Dix, who was even then rather tired from pushing seventy or so and inclined to be tart with young men eager to waste her time in taverns.

Luis spoke excellent English. The revolution had driven the Treviños with many other families to take refuge in the United States when Luis, the fifth son, was about eight. He had gone to school in Texas and Indiana, where he eventually dominated English in all but two particulars. The little confusion persists to this day: he cuffs when he has a cold on his chest, and due to the criminal negligence of his wife, the coughs of his shirts are frequently frayed.

We bade the Furlongs farewell. I was turned over to the vaccination, immigration, and customs authorities, and at last, in a car which had been provided by the Chamber of Commerce, complete with chauffeur, we set out for Monterrey. I had my hair tied up in a scarf and I was wearing a large black hat as well as sun glasses. Now the sun began to go down and long violet shadows crept across the plain. I took off my hat.

"Ah," breathed Luis.

I undid the scarf.

"So?" remarked Luis.

I took off the black glasses.

"Wonderful," he decided, aloud. He leaned toward me and looked at me soulfully.

"Shall I sing you a song about love?" he asked.

"Why yes," I agreed, thinking this must be a gag.

But he launched into "Palm Trees Drunk with the Sun," went on to "The Sea Gulls," and then sang "The Green Eyes," in a light baritone voice.

"Very nice," commented the chauffeur from the front seat. "Now sing 'Farolito.' "

He sang it. After our beer in Vallecillo, Luis sang other songs. He sang all the way to Monterrey.

I didn't realize it, but I was being courted.

On a high place, before we dropped down into another valley, we could see the far-off lights of Monterrey.

"That's it! There's Monterrey!" breathed Luis. "Isn't it beautiful?"

Like most Mexicans, he is passionately devoted to his *patria chica*, his *tierra*, the place where he was born.

As the days went by and I was busy gathering material for articles, Luis, acting for the Chamber of Commerce, arranged my interviews for me and when necessary interpreted for me. I had studied Spanish, and Mexicans are extraordinarily kind and patient with anyone who is trying to speak their language. I suspect that I needed the interpreter more than I knew. But through all this Luis frequently made me stop and admire the Saddle Mountain, which dominates the town with its curious, almost grotesque shape. The Saddle Mountain is beloved of the Monterrey people; when far from it they dream of it, but always they speak of it with deep sentiment. Luis wanted to arouse this devotion to his mountain in me. I should have realized that his interest was more than the routine politeness of the public-relations expert. It would have been clear to anyone but a candid American, when he made a detour to show me the *ranchito* of his father and mother, their summer and week-end place, a lovely rustic spot with a swimming pool under the pecan trees.

"What's that?" I asked, pointing to a field which glistened white as snow and moved softly in the breeze.

"Those are the *margaritas* (daisies) of Mamacita," smiled Luis. "She loves this flower, so when Papacito bought the ranch, he planted an acre of them for her, and when they were high, he brought her here to see them."

I was touched.

"You will meet Mamacita tonight," he told me.

This was tantamount to a proposal, but again, I didn't know the customs and I didn't realize that showing me to Mamacita was crucial.

I had finished my work in Monterrey and Luis had invited me to go out dancing. I accepted with alacrity, thinking this to be one more polite gesture from the public-relations department. But when he called for me at my hotel he was nervous; he mopped his forehead, he passed a long brown forefinger around the inside of his collar. He looked me over very carefully. I was wearing a long cotton dancing dress, with a neck and sleeves. This was fortunate; Luis sighed with relief. Rather pale with the pallor of the South Spanish type, the pallor described by Garcia Lorca as "olive and jasmin kneaded together," he led me out to where a lady sat in a car. She was, I thought, in early middle age; there was not one silver thread in the dark curling hair piled high on her head. In truth, she had just turned sixty. She was very plump and firm in a dark voile dress, and an incredibly small fat hand like a baby's manipulated her fan. Around her shoulders was a dark lace scarf. She smiled, showing tiny even white teeth.

"Mamacita," said Luis in slow English, "this is Eleesabet."

Very large eyes, wise and sparkling, looked me over, a dimple popped in and out. She had a great sense of fun, and she enjoyed teasing, a strong Mexican characteristic. She was teasing Luis, for she knew he hung on her judgment.

"I do not spik Eengleesh," she offered at last in a deep contralto.

In my careful Spanish I said that I was delighted to meet her, and her black brows arched with surprise and pleasure. She turned on Luis and gave him a short thorough tongue lashing, fanning very fast. Evidently he hadn't told her that the "mees" knew Spanish. She then made a place for me in the car at once and asked me in rapid succession my father's name and age, my mother's name and age, where I had studied Spanish and if it were true that Chile Tem-play (Shirley Temple) was really a dwarf.

We deposited Mamacita at a *cine,* or movie, where a small nephew was awaiting her, and then we went to collect another *pareja* or couple.

They proved to be special friends of Luis, a young

lawyer who knew English well enough to have acted a season of Shakespeare in the States, and a slim girl with dead black hair and a camelia-fair complexion, who had been to schools in San Antonio. They were Alejandro and Mercedes, and they were engaged.

We went to the Jardines de Terpsicore. These were gardens in very truth. A paved space was arranged for dancing among the trees. A fountain splashed at one end of the dancing pavilion, near the bandstand, and dozens of large crystal parasols shattered the moonlight into rainbow colors.

Luis is a wonderful dancer and I have always been an enthusiastic one. Only already well into the evening did it occur to me to wonder why we never exchanged dances with Alejandro and Mercedes. But we didn't. Alejandro and Mercedes gyrated past us; we swooped around them. All evening. Between dances we drank the clean bright-tasting Monterrey beer. We had a sandwich. At half-past eleven Mercedes revealed that her Mamacita had given permission only until this hour, and we must go at once. We took her home, and waited until the big gate had swung inward to receive her. She disappeared into the flower-filled patio, and we heard her call in Spanish. "It is I, Mamacita! I am home!"

I was left at my hotel. But a sort of die had been cast. Luis had cast it and with his eyes open. He had taken a strange woman to dance. Just any strange woman, and the incident might have been passed over as a wild oat on the part of the fifth Treviño. But he had taken the strange woman in company with a *pareja* of his best friends, an engaged couple! Two plus two equals four. Dancing with one girl all evening, with an engaged *pareja* to make up the party, means something serious! Phones rang in Monterrey; the news went round. Only I was in the dark.

Formally on the afternoon of the next day, I was taken to call on Mamacita. While we sat in the *sala*, Luis disappeared, to return with a tray on which sat Mamacita's best small silver liqueur glasses. In each was a thimbleful of sweet vermouth. On a plate were some little yellow cakes that melted into a puff of flavor when bitten. These were Mamacitas famous *polvorones de maizena* (cornstarch puff cookies), the engagement cake. Angelita, now married to Ernesto, had tasted these; they had been served the night Roberto asked for Adela's hand; they had been baked and sent to the family of Leonor when she became engaged to Ricardo. They were a kind of symbol. All unknowing I ate the engagement cakes and tasted the engagement vermouth.

Later Luis brought me a small yellow-striped kitten and dropped it into my lap.

"Oh, the darling! I wish I could have him," I cried. "But I am leaving tomorrow for Mexico City and I have lots of work to do. I won't be home in California for weeks."

Mamacita said calmly, "Galatea has kittens like these every four months. You will have a kitten."

Paling visibly, Luis scooped up the kitten and left. I wondered what had happened, but it seemed he had only recognized his mother's acceptance of me. Mamacita had decided that I was to come to Monterrey, marry Luis, and receive a kitten from the fecund Galatea. He had been working toward this, but it was serious and it sobered him to realize that he was practically a married man.

He came back to the *sala*, a formal somber room, with dark furniture upholstered in violet velvet, and sat down at the piano where he began to sing and play.

Mamacita listened a while and then confided to me, softly, so that he couldn't hear, "He is good. Noble. I never had any problems with Luis. Just the piano, to sing with, this is his vice."

I made my farewells and went back to my hotel to pack. That evening Luis called on me accompanied by his older brother Ernesto. There seemed to be little to say. But it was part of the pattern Luis followed faithfully, though I did not know it. In the absence of Papacito, who was out of town, Ernesto, oldest brother, must meet Eleesabet.

Next day at noon I took the train for Mexico City. Luis, in white pants, a dark blue coat, and the *jipi-japa*, saw me off. He was speechless. I got aboard the train and wondered why I felt so sad. I sat down and dropped a tear for pleasant friends I would not see again for a long time. The train started.

About fifteen minutes later the train slowed down and stopped for a moment and suddenly Luis burst into the Pullman coach like a tornado. He seized me and kissed me thoroughly, and I thought in the midst of a turmoil of emotion, "Why it's impossible! I've only known him a week!"

Luis got off the train, still having said nothing to me, but he looked very happy as he waved goodbye. He had driven madly and flagged the train to a stop. I still didn't know it, but I was an engaged woman.

Luis made this clear to me in his letters which followed me faithfully to every stop I made in the next year's wanderings, to California, across the country, and back to California again.

How many times I was to dance under the crystal parasols, how often I would tell Mamacita the true age of the stars of the screen, and learn from her wondrous recipes, written down by Doña Dolores, Mamacita's own grandmother's mother! How often we served the sweet vermouth, and *polvorones* I had learned to bake, never as good as Mamacita's!

Just how does a place, at first new and strange, come to take on a beloved familiarity? Living in another country, with people of another upbringing, under new sets of traditions, speaking another language, at what moment does one suddenly feel that he has fallen into place and is no longer alien?

It happens imperceptibly.

There comes a time when unconsciously one slips into thinking in the language so painfully learned from books, when the pattern of one's thoughts grows naturally from the first strange but dutifully accepted premise, into a new design. There is a moment when suddenly all that was outlandish, quaint, and exotic, is restored to strangeness only by the amazed comments of visitors from afar.

The somber *sala* came to be as dear to me as the water-green walls of the living room of my childhood, and the houses flush with the street as familiar as the tree-bordered lawns of the town where I grew up.

Galatea had only four more sets of yellow tiger kittens before she produced the batch from which I, a bride of days, selected Policarpo, most beloved of all the cats I ever owned. And long before Galatea had been gathered to her fathers, all that once had been so excitingly different and maddening and fascinating and queer, had become simply "home."

II

MY FATHER was molding bullets at the kitchen stove when I said to him, "Papa, I am going to marry a Mexican."

I can still remember the smell of the hot lead. I can see my father (always so impeccably dressed in the courtroom) clad now in his red lumberjack shirt and khaki trousers, his regular Saturday afternoon costume for relaxing.

"Does your mother know about this?"

"Yes."

There was a long silence while Papa thoughtfully molded half a dozen bullets.

"There's one thing you'll have to remember," he said, at last. "People get more so, as they grow older. You'll get more American; he'll get more Mexican."

"He's coming all the way here to see me. If you don't like him, I want you to tell me so."

"I will tell you."

As good luck (or bad) would have it, when Luis finally arrived, after countless letters and several false starts (to this day, he almost goes out of his mind when faced with a journey of even two or three hours' duration), I was out, having gone to have my hair done, for I was expecting him on the next day, Sunday. But Papa was home, and was arrayed to go hunting. To Luis' consternation, the door of the Borton menage was opened by a man in a red shirt, with a red bandana around his head, and a rifle in his hand.

Always afterwards Luis referred to my father affectionately as *Papá de la carabina,* meaning roughly, "Shotgun Papa."

Luis drew himself up staunchly and said, "I have come to marry Eleesabet."

Papa said, "She expected you tomorrow, and there's nobody home. I was about to go target shooting. Care to come along?"

Luis was wearing a pearl-gray suit and hat, and a gray satin tie, in which glowed an amethyst stick pin. He bowed and replied, "With pleasure!"

They got into Papa's hunting truck and drove away, Papa's dog Pooch on the front seat with them.

My father was a brilliant lawyer, famous for his courtroom technique, sought after as a public speaker. But he was inclined to judge a man on whether he knew how to follow deer trail and kill clean. Luis was being marched right up to a he-man test, in his pearl gray clothes, and his amethyst.

Papa was such a crack shot that he had been barred from all turkey shoots and other such competitions, for people would not buy tickets if F. E. Borton was allowed to compete. So he was relegated to target practice and squirrel shooting on Saturday afternoons.

At home later, pleasantly jittering about in expectation of the arrival of my fiancé next day, I looked out of the window and, when I saw my father and Luis and Pooch drive up in the truck, I almost fainted. They came in together, my father's arm proudly around Luis's shoulders. Still spotless, with his elegant hat on his black curls at just the correct angle, Luis had followed my father shot for shot, never surpassing him, never falling behind.

Luis also was a crack shot, but he had never happened to mention it to me. My father decided that I would be in good hands.

(I learned later that Luis had spent two years on horseback as paymaster for the Southern Pacific when the lines were being built through the wild country of Sonora and Jalisco, where Indians are still unreconstructed, and where paymasters are crack shots or find themselves officiating as corpses in funeral services.)

Luis had gained a powerful friend in my father, who went so far as to give him expert advice on how to manage me.

"She's amiable," said Papa, "and if you praise her often, you'll have no trouble with her. Watch her keys and valuables, for she's very absent-minded. But never put a bit on her, because if you do, she will simply buck herself to death."

But if Luis had a strong support in my father, I had a passionate friend, admirer, and defender in Mamacita.

After our marriage in California, we drove to Monterrey. We arrived late in the evening, and I was weary and suddenly a trifle frightened. The quiet streets of the Mexican town, the houses like fortresses along the narrow sidewalks, the barred windows, had an element of menace.

But Mamacita clasped me with such a bright smile of welcome, and around the table were ranged the merry faces of all the Treviños. I was so tired that I didn't understand a word of the Spanish, but I understood the significance of the special gift that Mamacita brought out for me.

During our wedding journey, when we had talked of countless things and had tried to catch each other up on the past, Luis had told me of his family's troubles during the Revolution. They had fled, leaving everything, and they had lost everything. Mamacita, brought up to many servants, had wept like a baby when faced with the washing for nine boys, her husband and daughter. She who had never stepped her tiny foot into a kitchen except to cajole her favorite dishes from the cook, had had to learn, tearfully and painstakingly, how to cook the beans and rice. Through all the hard times, through days bewilderedly learning basic English, sometimes going without food, while the Revolution raged, she had kept two little last bits of jewelry with her . . . a garnet cross that had been her mother's, and a jet cross edged with seed pearls that the camellia-skinned Doña Dolores, her great-grandmother, had worn to Mexico from Spain, as a bride.

"*Bienvenida* (welcome), Eleesabet," said Mamacita, and she fastened a chain around my neck.

I looked down and saw that shining against my travel-stained blouse I was wearing the jet cross of Dolores.

III

IN MY IGNORANCE and vanity I supposed that I would have no trouble with the language at all. My interviews when working had gone off reasonably well, and I had read large sections of *Don Quixote*. Once I had been hauled away from the Music Department of my paper to help report a murder case because the note found near the body had been written in Spanish. I considered myself a master of the tongue.

But I hadn't counted on several unknown factors. First, when in a group, Mexicans all talk at the same time and at the top of their lungs. Second, half the words are left out and special gestures take their place. To understand these you have to learn the whole lexicon of what is meant by each movement of shoulders, hands, wrists, eyebrows, forehead, and head. Third, Mexicans use a full vocabulary of words of Indian origin which the pompous Spanish Academy has not yet admitted to be a part of the living language, words which therefore are not to be found in any Spanish dictionary.

That night when I arrived in Monterrey, the entire Treviño clan available in Monterrey was ranged round the banquet table. There were Papacito and Mamacita, Tia Maria, six brothers and their wives, and families, and

Adela and her husband and family. Plus three servants and a set of hysterical dogs.

The blast of welcoming Spanish almost knocked me off my feet. Luis made them be silent while I gathered my wits and pronounced an answer in precise and elegant Castilian. This was received with hearty and spontaneous laughter.

Though I had taken honors in Spanish in college, my Mexican family made it clear, as the days went by, that the most amusing and endearing thing about me was the inherent entertainment in my Spanish. But Papacito protected me from too much good-natured wit at my expense by correcting carefully and with the greatest kindness, all my errors, and by teaching me a beautiful precept.

"Never worry about your accent, Eleesabet," he said. "You will always have one. But if you speak a correct Spanish, the accent will be a charm. But do not use the Castilian mannerisms here, just as I would not try to use an Oxford English in Texas, with my Mexican accent. How would I sound asking for petrol instead of gas and trying to say Thenks veddy moch. Drop the theta. But never use any slang."

The "theta" is the Spanish lisped c or z. In Mexico these letters are pronounced like s.

Little by little I learned to be correct if not affected in my Spanish, to use idioms and the vivid expressions which were not vulgar. Papacito watched over me and prevented me from taking up such interesting, though incorrect, Indian circumlocutions as repetition for stress, as "The girl is pretty pretty pretty!" and the strange (and much used) "The water is boil boil" (instead of "boiling,") or "The baby is cry cry."

Nevertheless, I went one day to the butcher shop and asked for something in such a way as to entirely unhinge the butcher. He leaned on his chopping block, shaking with laughter, while tears streamed down his face, and he was so weakened he could not even wield his cleaver. What I said I do not know to this day.

And for years I had an attack of nerves every time Spanish came at me out of a phone.

Mamacita and Papacito addressed me in the familiar second person, as *tu*. But I always spoke to them, as did all their children, in the third person formal *usted* or "your mercy."

However, I had not been taught the *tu* or second person of verbs, when I learned Spanish, as it was thought we would never need these forms. I therefore always addressed my husband as "his mercy," and the word got round that Luis was awfully severe with his wife, and maybe even beat her in private.

In Monterrey some words which are obsolete in modern Spanish persist in the language. They were brought there four centuries ago by the Spanish conquerors, and are still "alive" linguistically. One hears ancient verb forms of the word "to bring," and some words like *parian* instead of *mercado* for market, and *azotea* instead of *terraza* for terrace. There are many others.

At the same time, Americanisms have crept in with *beesquites* (biscuits), *jot queques* (hot cakes) and the like, and in the train of baseball, a series of *jon rons, auts,* and *jits. Uiski* (whiskey) is a favorite drink, in a *jaibol.* (J is pronounced like h.) *Esueteres* are knitted for one's children in the winter, and in the summer one can buy an *escuna* (schooner) of beer.

But Monterrey held pitfalls in a part of the language I never dreamed of. These were the names.

My husband's father's name was Porfirio Treviño Arreola. But, as he was an engineer, he was frequently addressed as "Señor Ingeniero," and Mamacita was called then *la señora del ingeniero,* or "the engineer's lady." My husband's name is Luis Treviño Gómez, for Mamacita's name as a girl had been Adelita Gómez Sánchez; on her marriage she became Adelita Gómez de Treviño. It will be seen that children use the father's name first and the mother's name last. Women keep their maiden name intact, merely adding "de" (belonging to) and the husband's name. Thus I became Elizabeth Borton de Treviño. Properly written in the old Spanish style, my name would have carried both my father's and mother's names, and also my husband's father's and mother's names, thus: Mary Elizabeth Victoria (my full baptismal name) Borton Christensen de Treviño Gómez. Sounds complicated, but it has the virtues of complete orientation.

For example, let us suppose two young things are rattling on about Pepe Morones. Their mother, to get it straight, stops them and says, "Whom do you mean?" The reply is his full name. "José de Jesus Morones Maldonado." "Ah," thinks Mamacita. "They mean the son of Adalberto Morones Calderon, who married Concha Maldonado Becerra." Everything is cleared up.

My name in Spanish is Isabel and I asked Mamacita if she did not want to call me that. Or Chavela, the nickname.

"No," she said firmly. "To Luis you are Eleesabet, so to us all, you will be Eleesabet."

My kind sister-in-law Adela (who was often called

"Nena" or Girlie), arranged a dancing party in our honor at the Terpsicore Gardens, to introduce me to her friends. About fifty couples had been invited. My head began to swim after the third introduction and by the end of the evening I was lost. I had met Sr. de la Garza y Garza, Sr. Garza Gonzalez, Sr. Gonzalez Garza, Sra. Gonzalez de Garza y Garza, Nena Garza de Gonzalez, Sr. Treviño Garza, Sr. Treviño Gonzalez-Garza, Nena Garza de Treviño, Sra. Treviño de Treviño, and so on and so on, mostly Garza Gonzalez and Treviño in endless combinations. These happen to be the most common family names in Monterrey, and each family is much intermarried with the others, and all are prolific.

I said to Adela, "I am done for. I'll never remember *anybody's* name. Whatever shall I do?"

"Just speak to everybody you see, and say *Adios,*" she advised me.

But I protested. I had studied enough Spanish to know that *adios* means "Goodbye."

"Oh, but you wouldn't say it like that, '*adios,*' meaning 'Goodbye,'" explained Adela, horrified. "You say it this way. '*Adiooooooos?*' That way it means 'Hello!'"

IV

THERE ARE a number of charming "colonias" or residence sections in Monterrey, many of them modern and very much in the American style, but I had fallen in love with Mamacita's old-fashioned Mexican house, and I wanted a patio, and barred windows, and a fountain. She was against this idea, for she loved everything bright and new, herself. But at last I found a little house which had everything I had been looking for except the fountain. The barred windows curved outward in a very pregnant manner, the floors were all tiled in a pattern of rust and gray, and there were *two* patios. My address: Morelos 829. Here I lived the early years of my marriage.

The rooms closed with great wooden shutters against the dangerous night air, and the *dispensa* or food-storage room, and the kitchen and dining room were divided from each other by long windy corridors. But though these arrangements had certain disadvantages, there is no tranquility quite equal to that of a garden within high walls, where you can wander barefoot in your nightgown on a heavenly summer morning.

I had to achieve my garden with the help of many potted ferns and plants, since my patio was entirely paved, but before long I had a kind of thick flowering jungle there. Climbing vines twisted everywhere and hung down over the recessed doorways.

In Monterrey homes the *dispensa* is supposed to be locked, to prevent pilfering of rice and sugar by the servants, and the ice box (almost always kept in the dining room) is also padlocked against possible lowering of the level in the milk bottles, and other depredations. Keys to all these things, plus keys to the silver drawer and dish closets, to the linen press, to the clothes closets and trunks and desks are supposed to hang from the belt of the lady of the house. Not for nothing is she known in Spanish as *ama de llaves,* or keeper of the keys. As I lost all my keys frequently, we soon gave up and left ourselves to chance, and the servants took good care of my treasures because the *señora* was so evidently less than capable.

It took us months to save up enough money to buy curtain material for the eleven fifteen-foot high windows, and I slowly collected the indispensable implements of housekeeping . . . the mops and buckets, the wash board, feather dusters on very long poles, and the sundry gourds, clay cooking vessels, scraps of rope which were used as dish scourers and many strange vegetables which served as soap, scouring pads, and hot-dish protectors. A root called *amole* is soaked in water to generate rich suds that wash floors without leaving any scum, the dried membranes of certain squashes make wonderful dish cloths, and little pats of earth molded into cakes serve to clean brass and copper.

My *sala* or living room was furnished for some time exclusively with a small Rosencranz piano which I had found for sale in a poor section of the city. It had been made in 1840 before Mr. Edison, and had two small candle-holders flanking the portrait of Mozart just above the music rack. Several thousand generations of cockroaches and crickets rioted in its insides, but I fumigated it and bought it new felts, and it has gladdened my home ever since.

I had been given presents of money with which to buy linens and dishes, and Mamacita offered to help me shop for them. I wanted bright Mexican woven cottons and the brilliant glazed ware of Oaxaca and Guadalajara. Mamacita was horrified; only Indians and poor people used that stuff. She marched me straight to Monterrey's best home-furnishings store, and made sure I bought correct Czecho-Slovakian and English china and glass. She herself gave me fine white damask tablecloths.

Many years later she visited an old friend in Mexico City, a lady famous for her chic and elegance, and was seated at luncheon at a table set with Mexican pottery and blue glass. Overcome with remorse as she remembered my tastes, she rushed out and bought me the country-style things I admired, to atone. But of course her resistance to the cheap hand-made native crafts was typical of provincial Mexican elegance at the time. Even today, it is mostly folk-lore conscious foreigners and "arty" people who use the native goods in their homes. Mexicans like fine French and Spanish furniture, the most delicate of Limoges china, and Persian rugs. But the strong hand of the United States is to be seen in the bathrooms and the kitchens.

Of tremendous importance in setting up housekeeping in Mexico are the servants. Life is geared to them and since every home employs at least two, and since their families and relatives are regularly succored, hospitalized, dosed, fed and loaned money, one performs a sort of private social service in hiring them.

Instead of the vacuum cleaner, the washing machine, and the mangle, you have Lupe and Torquata and Tencha. Instead of packaged mixes and frozen foods and things in cellophane, you have a Chonita who goes out every day with her basket and the *gasto* which is the daily allowance for food. With this she travels to the market and buys everything, haggling and pinching and tasting and enjoying a good chat with her friends. Then she comes home and contrives three meals for her *patrona* and the family, herself and the other servants, and all their relatives and friends who may drop in.

Even baby sitters are unknown, for as soon as a new baby arrives in any family a new *nana* (nurse) or *pilmama* (an Indian word for wet nurse) is hired, whose duties are to tend the baby, wash and feed him, change him, entertain him, love him, take care of all his clothes, and if necessary, feed him at the breast. In Mexico a good clean fat *pilmama* is infinitely preferred to a formula, by parents in general, and always by the baby. So tremendously important is the *pilmama* or *nana* that she, as much as the ubiquitous mother-in-law, is often the cause of domestic struggles between husband and wife. I have known wives to flounce home to mother until their husbands got rid of the nana who had brought them up and was still a power.

Mamacita gave me sage advice about hiring servants, but wisely did not hire for me herself, for servants obey and respect the person who engages them and pays them. Therefore I had to do the hiring in order to be in a position to fire as well, if this seemed to be indicated. Mexican servants wisely recognize only one boss.

"For cook," Mamacita told me, "choose a woman who

is fat, for this means that she is probably healthy and likes to eat. If she likes to eat she will taste the food as it cooks and season it properly. Beware these thin women who cook with disdain, for they don't make anything taste good. "But for your housemaid, choose a *solterona* (old maid), if you can find one. They are slightly embittered at life for having passed them by and they take out their frustrations in cleaning and scrubbing. Also, they keep a sharp and envious eye on the other servants and have them all terrified of their tongues, so they keep a house in order. Never hire a young and pretty girl for housemaid, for they spend their time at the window looking for their sweetheart, and playing the radio when you are out, and they steal your powder and perfume."

My first servants all drifted away from me after a few months, dispite my tearful pleadings, giving me one vague excuse or another or none, until it became apparent, even to the most myopic, that there was going to be an heir in the house of the fifth Treviño. Then all the servants came back to me, smiling, patted my protuberance affectionately, and were eager to work for me again, since they were now assured that I wasn't one of those crazy foreign women who didn't want children. No one cared to endure the bad luck of working in a house unblessed by the patter of little feet and the lusty squalling that makes the whole world kin. "It was too quiet, too sad," they all told me. "But now that there will be a *niño!* Maybe even twins. . . ." And their eyes shone with anticipation.

In my earliest days as a *señora* I was troubled because I didn't know how to arrange the meals. I had to learn that one always began with a *sopa*, which is a dish made of rice,

macaroni, or some paste; then went on to meat and vegetables and salad, and finally to dessert. And always, after
the meat, the beans. No butter was to be served, but
instead, always, there must be a *salsa*—a sharp sauce of
tomatoes and chile—and various spices. At first I had to
throw myself on the mercy of the servants, in planning
dinners that my husband would eat, and one servant left
me in disgust, complaining to Mamacita that the little
señora didn't know how "to command."

Another maid was almost too religious for me, though
Mamacita had told me to be sure to hire a pious girl and
let her go daily to mass and Rosary.

This girl was Tomasa.

I asked her, "Can you make bread, muffins, cookies?"

"God willing," she answered.

I hired her, and she spent the first day arranging her
room, nailing up pictures of all her favorite saints, her little
basin of Holy Water, and a small altar where she installed
the Holy Family with candles and flowers.

Whenever I asked her to make a dish she didn't know
she would crash right down on her knees and ask God to
send her the recipe. Usually He did and very good recipes
too, though He is fonder of lard than I am. Whenever she
served the table she would pause in the doorway of the
dining room, roll her eyes heavenward and say aloud,
"Dios Mio, please don't let the *señora* criticize this dish, for
You know how I burnt my finger and what a chore it is to
grind up all those *chiles* anyhow."

This always effectively silenced me, especially as it was
also her practice, when setting a dish before me, to make
the sign of the cross above it, but one day my husband
dared to protest against one of the holy recipes, and

Tomasa left us never to return, declaring she couldn't outrage her immortal soul by working for heathens.

Some servants are very sensitive and take umbrage at the most innocent of actions or gestures. Luis and I often conversed in English, with the result that one little maid left me and ran home to her mother, reporting that the *señores* were always saying things about her in Arabic. I was startled until Luis explained that among the country people *Arabe* means any heathen tongue, and when they say to anyone, "Say it in Christian!" it means "Speak Spanish!"

In those early days when I had so much to learn, the servants were very patient with me. Not one but served me tenderly as nurse whenever I was ill, no matter what her other duties; not one but brought me presents of flowers, vegetables, or handwork on my saint's day, even long after they had left my employ; and never did anyone leave me because of extra work caused by my children and my varied and maddening animals.

One of them, Maria, hired as cook, took on the care of the plants as well, and cooked abstractedly, one eye on the traffic in the street. Whenever an *arriero* (muleteer) went by with his train of burros, she was out like a flash with broom and dustpan, sweeping up hot potent fresh manure for the finest flowers. She stole cuttings for me, and wheedled roots and slips from the gardeners in houses that had lawns, and from friends of hers who worked for other *señoras* who kept fine plants.

Servants are part of the fabric of my life in Mexico and I cannot think of life without them, and yet they are not an unmixed blessing. Hilaria, for instance.

Hilaria had an innocent interest in *muertitos* (the dead), and would leave work any time to attend a funeral, especially if it were the funeral of a child. Then she would weep luxuriously for days.

There was Nieves. Nieves was a maiden lady of a certain age, in my employ as housemaid. The passing years had not embittered her at all, but had caused her to grow only more coy and flirtatious. Every afternoon she would pose in a window, with a rose in her graying hair, inviting passing workmen and startled gentlemen bound for home and supper, to "fly to the bosom of their dove" and she would indicate her own ample bosom.

There was Teresa who nearly committed suicide with my husband's pistol because her sweetheart (a policeman) hadn't phoned when he said he would. That is, she grabbed the gun, which Luis kept on the top shelf in his closet, roared that she was going to blow her brains out, and almost did, had it not been for my washwoman who threw herself into the fray and fought with her. The gun went off, and the bullet went through the door of my children's bedroom.

I have learned a lot from my maids, especially humility, one of the Christian virtues to which I never gave much thought in my heedless youth. Once I would have felt superior to an illiterate; our education teaches us many such vain assumptions. But I learned that all my illiterate servants have, in general, excellent memories that would put to shame the writers (and readers!) of "Improve Your Memory" books. They could give me long complicated messages without an error, and could do sums in their heads faster than I can with pencil, paper, and eraser.

They have an intellectual integrity formed by their own experiences at first hand, unadulterated by watered-down and half-understood ideas at second hand, or from reading ideologies and printed manifestos foreign to their life and setting. They are capable of very sensible judgments because they have never learned to mix their thoughts with "escape literature."

One maid, Severia, asked permission to go to a meeting which had been organized by a *lider* (leader) in order to form the servant girls into a union. What this meeting was, and who the *lider* was I do not know, but Severia came home with the report that it had been proposed in the meeting that one day all the servants would expropriate their patron's house, just as the government had expropriated the oil of the foreign companies in Mexico.

"And what do you think of this plan, Severia?" I asked.

"Well, *señora*, it doesn't sound practical to me. It is all very well for me to expropriate your house, with the *dispensa* full of rice and beans and lard. But when they are gone, who will buy me more? Not you, for I can scarcely expect you to give me your kitchen and also a salary. So where would I be, then? No, *señora*, and not even the government would give me the rice and beans, for I have heard government promises before. So, if you are willing, let us continue as we were, I cook for you, and you pay me my salary. Agreed?"

I agreed.

I was wringing my hands and worrying about world troubles one day when Severia asked me why I was afflicting myself. I explained to her about what bad things were being done all over the globe.

"Señora, you go to mass, you are a Catholic, are you not? Do not think about those bad people, *señora*, God will attend to them in his own good time. I am certain of this, for there must have been many bad times before, and yet here we are, you and I, are we not?"

I am inclined to think Severia's solution of the world's ills may, in the eye of Time, have as much sense to it, and more, as the drastic remedies we have often recommended, and sometimes take.

V

THE STRANGEST thing about my new life, at first, was getting used to the sounds. I had long been conditioned to the morning roar of trucks up the hill, the clatter of milk cans, the underground thunder of subways, ceaseless hooting of automobile horns. Now I heard the solemn pealing of church bells through the long sleepy afternoons, the early-morning chants of ambulatory vendors, laughing of burros, scolding of parrots in near-by patios, distant or closer music of serenaders.

My little house on Morelos Street was half a block from the cathedral. At five in the morning deep-toned bells rumbled through the half dark calling to early mass. The bells toll a constant clangor, then pause a moment, and peal once. This means, "First call. You have thirty minutes to get up and get dressed and get here." Fifteen minutes later the same clangor, then two single peals, well spaced. "Second call. You should be putting on your mass veil, taking up your rosary and prayer book, for you have only fifteen minutes to run through the gray light toward the dark bulk of the church." Then comes the last clangor and three peals. Mass is about to begin. Preceded by his altar boys, the priest is about to go up to the altar.

The mellow-toned bells rang for mass all the morning.

29

In the afternoon they called to Rosary and Holy Hour. And sometimes they tolled mournfully for funeral masses. In times gone by, the big bell in the church tower called people to the square to hear important news; if that great bell were to clang imperiously and continuously even now, the people would congregate in the plaza, wondering and fearful, to learn what had happened.

And all day a small clear-voiced bell in one tower sounded the quarter hours. Wakeful in the dark at night, I could hear them; they sounded through the dreams of my luxurious siestas; all day I heard the bells, as I went about my tasks or sat to read. They sounded, marking the hours that fled. At first they made me nervous and sad. Later I loved them, for they marked happiness into portions I could perceive. They urged me, without ceasing, to laugh, to appreciate, to love, for Time is always passing.

In Mexico dogs are often quartered on the flat roofs, and they are officious guardians, always barking ferociously, promising dire death to any character passing below in the streets who looks or smells unacceptable. Turkeys are penned on the roofs to fatten them, and their hungry early-morning gobbling is a typical sound.

The vendors have their chants or songs; you tell your servant to go out to buy bread or fruit or *aguamiel* (fresh-pressed sugarcane juice, a morning pick-me-up) according to whose song you have recognized. Some of these songs are charming, little poems in tone; most of them are unforgettable. The sharpener of scissors and knives has his chant; the man who drives donkeys laden with black loam and leaf mold his melody; the bread man, with a great basket shaped like a hat on his head, the upturned brim filled with fresh hot loaves and fancy sweet buns, or *pan dulce,* has a queer snorting cry I would recognize in the middle of Africa.

And there are other sounds, according to the time of day.

In the earliest hours and late at night, besides the cries of the vendors, there is the ever-present sharp neat patter of burro hooves against the paved and cobble-stoned streets, the occasional shout of *"Arre, burro!"* and the always wonderfully amusing and touching braying of a garrulous donkey, temporarily tethered outside some home while the owner bargains out a sale of wood or vegetables.

Mexican provincial families know there are such things as insane asylums but they do not let such institutions enter into their lives in any way. Unless you are absolutely indigent, and the state comes to take your *loquito* away from you, you care for him yourself. No one considers sending his afflicted away to those halls of loneliness and death. So it is that in provincial towns you sometimes hear wild laughter or formless muttering from inside some patio. I don't know the name of the sad old gentleman who lived in a house a few doors down from mine on the other side of the street. But I know the name of the wife he had loved so dearly that when she died he lost his mind. It was Carmela. All day he was happy at small tasks, making toys for his grandchildren, doing household errands, reading his prayer book. But with the falling dark, his loss would descend on him, and he would look for her through the window, and call her and call her, in a strong loud voice, infinitely despairing, for hours. "Carmela, Carmela!"

About five, when the houses would begin to stir with life after the absolute black out of the siesta, the piano practice begins. There are movies, radios, record players in Monterrey. But also there are pianos. It is considered an essential grace in the female to be able to play at least the easier waltzes of Chopin and piano teachers flourish as the green bay tree. Walking down any street you may pass house after house from which drift dreamy, determined, annoyed, or plodding versions of the "Moonlight Sonata" (as the character of the piano student imposes itself on his musical labors), and more or less recognizable mazurkas and preludes from the beloved "Cho-peen." Loud and fierce scales are performed, arpeggios, and all sorts of finger exercises. Piano teaching is stern and old-fashioned and the limp wrist and circling elbow are looked on with scorn.

Mamacita told me that in "the old days" there were always bands of *cieguitos* or blind men to play for dances or to serenade, but I never saw them. The old custom of Papacito lighting an after-dinner cigar and then saying to the son of the house to go out and look for the *cieguitos*, so that they might have a party, had more or less disappeared.

But I learned of two or three small groups of musicians who eke out a livelihood by means of the calendar and Mexican sentiment. What happens is more or less as follows: Let us suppose we waken to notice that it is the nineteenth of March. Now this is the day of San José (Saint Joseph), most chaste spouse of the Virgin. The musicians all know this and they have marked down the addresses of all the most important Jose's in the city. They go forth to waken these Joseph's with *mañanitas*, morning serenades, to honor their saint's day. Violins, guitars, a double-bass for thumping and plucking, and perhaps a clear-toned cornet. All the José's and Josefina's who have been accorded this fine and delicate courtesy of a morning serenade must respond with some slight monetary appreciation, or be known forever as clods. So it goes all year. But while the heaviest take is on days of very popular saints, like José, Juan, Francisco, Manuel, the two Luises (San Luis de Gonzaga, and San Luis Rey de Francia), Miguel, Pablo, Pedro, and others, no day need be a dead loss. In every town there is at least one Marcelino, Fernando, Emilio, Rosendo, Eduardo, Gonzalo. . . . Ladies, especially society leaders and wives of prominent officials, are serenaded too. You can hardly hear yourself think, at dawn on the days of Carmen, María, Dolores, Concepción, Mercedes, and Gloria, because of the serenades.

Composers need never starve either. They live not so much by the calendar of saints as by the social news. Every time a wedding is announced a really progressive composer produces for the bridegroom a song in praise of his beloved, weaving in her full name. If the music sounds a trifle like "Over the Waves" and one or two of Agustin Lara's latest, no matter. The touched young man must respond with a decent present, preferably folded into an envelope. And bridal marches elaborately dedicated to the happy pair being married are respectfully delivered to the home of the newly married couple and paid for (by the bridegroom). I myself have a copy of a strongly martial piece entitled "The Glorious Wedding Day of Luis and Elizabet." Luis paid twenty pesos for it. It is a fine piece, reminiscent of "Anchors Aweigh."

Band concerts take place for the promenade on Sunday evenings, to this day, for Monterrey is one of the few provincial towns that preserves the Sunday night circling of the plaza, to the strains of various offerings by the town band, which moves from plaza to plaza during the week, culminating in Zaragoza Plaza on Sunday.

And often through the soft evening air sounded the love-sick cadences of the lovers' serenades. Swains bring musicians to the barred windows of their adored ones, and often join in themselves, thus adding a note of genuine authenticity to the love songs. How often as I went to sleep, I heard the drifting strains of "Nunca, Nunca" ("Never, Never"), or "Los Ojos Verdes" ("The Green Eyes") along with the bells of the quarter hour and the moaning of the cat from the Chinese laundry who came often to yodel hopefully at my Policarpo and to stare at him with intense reproachful eyes. In the delicate Mexican expression, Policarpo had been "guaranteed."

VI

IN MY FIRST weeks and months in Monterrey, I was so busy learning the Mexican way of running a household and getting acquainted with Papacito and Mamacita and Luis's eight brothers and sister Adela, that I didn't realize that I was being snubbed. I was. No one came to call on me except the wife of the American vice-consul (dear Penny!) and I made no Mexican friends. This was because, in the tight social organization of a Mexican provincial town, where courtship is a long process, a dance with intricate steps, in which everything must be done according to tradition, I had blithely spoiled the pattern.

I, an interloper, a foreigner, had deprived some Monterrey *señorita* of a perfectly good husband. And a Monterrey man, who should have had to court and pass inspection and submit to the rules for at least two years, had got himself married with practically no trouble and in a matter of a few months, too! It was setting a terrible precedent, and we were let strictly alone, to teach us a lesson and to teach other Monterrey young men that such goings-on were not looked on kindly.

But when some months had gone by and it was observed that Luis was going to be a papa, hearts softened and we were forgiven. Besides, by that time Luis's youngest brother Roberto was involved in his unbelievable, fantastic, and very correct courtship of Beatriz. We were let off the hook.

One by one shy *señoritas* and *señoras* came to visit me, and when my first son Guicho, "The Little General," was born, I was "in."

But meanwhile I was occupied learning to shop and conducting my first quarrels with my husband. Matrimonial squabbles are always about 1. Love and/or 2. Money. In the love department we had no trouble. But we did a good deal of noisy adjusting to the problem of money. Right away we came up against the whole matter of the *gasto*.

Gasto means "expense" and is generally used to indicate exactly the sum set aside for the daily purchase of food and household necessities.

There may be a few Monterrey husbands, naturally careless fellows or contaminated by the United States, who turn over to their wives a fixed sum with which to run the house every month, or who even pass over to her their earnings so that she may control expenses, savings, and what-not. These are, in the cautious north of Mexico, a race as rare as hen's teeth. Most Monterrey men provide only the daily *gasto* and this is calculated with great cunning. As a matter of fact the custom has certain advantages even I can see.

Firstly, the little woman, who has always had a small daily amount of money to spend on fripperies from her papa, continues a habit she is used to. She is also made to watch where the money goes (easier taught with small sums) and is not tempted to make expensive down payments on floor-waxing machines and imported cake beaters.

One bride, who had never managed more than ten pesos in her life, was given three hundred pesos as a monthly *gasto* by her American husband and she so fell a prey to the first sales talk she had ever heard that she bought ten hams. In general, since Mexican women are reared under a heavy mantle of protection and are kept from harsh contacts with the voracious world of commerce, it is considered rash to give a woman as much as fifty pesos at a time. She is likely to plunge right out and buy a couple of hats or do something else equally foolish.

My *gasto* at first was three pesos a day, and was far beyond my station, as Luis' total monthly salary at that time amounted to three hundred pesos (at that time worth about eighty-five dollars). With my *gasto* I was supposed to buy meat, milk, vegetables and fruit, bread and such staples as sugar, rice, beans, and coffee. Luis had fixed the *gasto* after long worried discussions with Adela's husband, and they had calculated in a certain amount of slack because of my inexperience with Mexican ways. But I barely made ends meet and was constantly in a tearful turmoil because the cook would come and report that there was no lard or no rice or no eggs, after the shops had closed.

Luis was very patient with me, . . . at first. I so often had to borrow a *toston* (fifty centavos) against the next day's *gasto,* that he would frequently invite me out to supper in order to let me catch up with my debts. What upset him was that I would not bargain. But I couldn't. It embarrassed me to try. It gave me the feeling that I was supposed to do somebody out of a rightful profit, or let them do me out of some of Luis' money. Both ideas paralyzed me.

While I bought some groceries from a Spanish grocery shop, I was supposed to go to the big market, or "*parian*" as they call it in Monterrey, where, under one enormous roof, countless vendors had set up their stalls in a wild confusion of boxes and counters and noise and milling-about of people.

The market men soon sized me up. The Mexicans simply pretended not to understand my Spanish, or if they saw that I was determined to haggle, they began at a price about five hundred per cent higher than they were willing to settle for, and allowed me to beat them down a little.

The Chinese fruit and vegetable men confused me by saying my dialogue as well as their own.

"How much are string beans?" I would ask.

"Fifty centavos. Very expensive. The man must be crazy," they would reply.

There was nothing to do but pay the fifty cents or slink away.

My husband struggled to teach me proper procedure. The strongest lesson was administered when I bought the pineapple.

I had bought the blasted pineapple (after gritting my teeth and bargaining for the better part of half an hour) for a peso. When Luis saw the peso pineapple he struck his brow with the flat of his hand (a gesture which means "God help us all!") and said, "They take advantage of your blond hair. They think you are a *tourist!* Come. Watch me, and see how to do it."

He strode into the market with me some three or four abashed yards behind him. He went to the fruit stall and looked around scornfully, and then pushed a few fruits with a disdainful forefinger.

The vendor hurried over, snarling, "Don't touch, if you don't intend to buy!"

"Dirty place you have here," remarked Luis. "Look at that pile of peelings over in the corner. I must remember to tell the inspector."

"What inspector?"

"Treviño. My brother." (No brother was an inspector, but as there are thousands of Treviños in northern Mexico, there may well have been one who was an inspector.)

"I pay my license right on the dot!" defensively.

"But you've got some fruit there that ought to be condemned. Those pineapples, for instance."

"What? Those beautiful pineapples! They're worth a peso and twenty centavos apiece!"

Luis took a paper from his pocket and seemed to consult it.

"What's that?" Suspiciously, from the vendor.

"Government prices on fruit. Just a moment. I'm checking up on pineapples . . ."

"Look, I could let you have one for seventy centavos. As a favor."

"Apples, fifty centavos a kilo. Bananas . . . let's see now. . . ."

"Fifty centavos for a pineapple! I'm losing money, too."

Luis pretended to be momentarily interested.

"You mean one of those small pineapples over there? The ones that look bruised?" Incredulous.

"Well take them for forty centavos each. I haven't got all day."

Luis bought two pineapples for forty centavos each. He and the vendor parted full of mutual admiration.

I went over and held out my hand to Luis.

"How do you do?" I inquired. "Let me present myself. My name is Mrs. Mud."

That's how I lost the *gasto*. Luis turned it over to the cook. At the time, it seemed fair enough. But it hurt, all the same, to be demoted.

However, marriage is a game of give and take. I had taken a wallop. It was soon my turn to give one.

It happened this way.

The *gasto* was to cover purchases for food. But as time went by we began to need other things. Flea powder for Policarpo, the cat. Hairpins. Electric light bulbs. Dish towels. Tooth paste. Tacks. Shoe polish.

Luis said I had only to tell him what was needed and he would bring it from town. But I wanted to look in shop windows and wander in and out of stores. In short, I wanted to shop.

It went hard with me to ask for the money for each little item. So my list was rather extensive when I brought myself to present it. Luis went over it with some trepidation. It came to more than fifty pesos. An appalling sum.

"But I only earn three hundred pesos," he wailed. "And extra, with some commission I make. But I have to save the commissions for the baby. You can only buy one thing at a time." He gave me the exact amount indicated for the purchase of the first item on the list, Poli's flea powder.

I soon found that I was expected to wheedle the money for each purchase when the moment seemed propitious, beginning, "Lindo . . ." (which means "Pretty boy"). I refused to call Luis "Lindo." I refused to coax and plead and kiss for what I thought I should have proffered me as a right. Mexican women go through the little form, Mexican men adore the game. But I was a hard-headed foreigner.

I stamped my foot. I demanded a charge account.

Luis almost fell dead. Only very rich people had charge accounts. Nobody would let us open one; we weren't important enough.

Finally we worked out a compromise. Luis said I could go to the shops and choose what was needed and sign a "*vale*" for it. (A *vale* is a sort of IOU, a chit.) This sounded to me rather like an honorable charge account, so I agreed. Next day after siesta, I went to a shop and bought face powder and soap and signed a *vale*, and to another shop where I bought two meters of unbleached muslin and some thread and signed a *vale*. I window-shopped luxuriously and arrived home about an hour later. Two young men were guarding my door. They were holders of the *vales* I had signed. They demanded immediate payment. I had no money and Luis wasn't home. We had a dramatic scene in broken English and broken Spanish and several varieties of dirty looks were exchanged. This occurred at about five in the afternoon.

At five-thirty the shop owners phoned to ask me when I intended to pay. At six both young men were back. But I had to report that my husband had not yet arrived. They acted as if they knew very well he was that moment hiding behind the door, but they left. At six thirty they were back. I wouldn't answer the door. At eight the next morning, they both appeared again, and presented the *vales*. Luis paid them both.

But I had had enough. I would sign no more chits, I said. I asked Luis for an allowance. He explained that this was not sensible; I might buy more than I needed.

"You treat me as if I had been locked up all my life like a Mexican girl!" I accused.

"I am not a rich American!" he countered.

"You are domineering and bossy!" I wept.

Then he shouted at me the worst epithet . . . the thing most horrible!

"You want to be *independent!*" he roared, and stormed out of the house.

What could I do? We had had a terrible, an awful quarrel. Luis had left the house in a temper. I was in tears. I did what any bewildered bride would do. I went home to Mama. But as my own mother was thousands of miles away, it was to Mamacita that I went with my tale of woe.

She listened to me. Then she laughed heartily. Then she suddenly got mad and said many things to herself in loud annoyed Spanish. Then she calmed down, and was very thoughtful for a while. Suddenly she patted me, and said, "*Yo voy arreglarlo.* I feex."

She went to her desk and wrote out a list of about fifty ten-centavo and twenty-centavo purchases. She also wrote out Luis's business address. Then she briefed me. I followed her instructions to the letter.

I made all the small purchases, one by one, and signed a vale for each, and directed the collector to Luis's office. All afternoon a parade of boys with chits passed through his office. All were so small that he couldn't refuse to pay. He couldn't do any work. He was interrupted every ten minutes. He was busy all afternoon paying for two quinine tablets, half a dozen hooks and eyes, twenty centavos of bicarbonate, one yard of white tape, four sheets of writing paper and two envelopes, etc., etc.

I waited for his return home in the evening with some uneasiness. It was just possible that he might be annoyed. But he walked in calmly and announced that he was going to give me an allowance. It would grow larger with his salary, when that grew.

"Santo Remedio" or Holy Remedy, as they say. I suspected that he had discerned the fine hand of Mamacita in the parade of boys with *vales*. But the dove of peace flew in the door of Morelos 829 once more and there were no more quarrels.

Eventually I learned all the weapons of bargaining, the look of scorn, the false starts away, the eyebrow lifting, the eyes rolled heavenward. I got the *gasto* back.

But I had learned a lesson too.

One has no rights with a Mexican husband. Mexican women flatter and tease and love them into generosity. Or they simply outwit them.

VII

IN MAMACITA'S *sala* hung an oil painting of one of Papacito's distinguished forbears in military uniform. Dashing Colonel Modesto Arreola, who had helped defeat the French at Puebla, during the war to throw out the French-army-sustained "empire" of the ill-fated Maximilian and Carlotta. It was a snub-nosed boyish face, *chapeado* or pink-cheeked, with light hazel-green eyes and curling brown hair. When I first met Luis's youngest brother Roberto (who had been so long in the United States that everybody called him Bob) I knew at once where I had seen him before. He was *Modesto Arreola* to the life.

Bob had been engaged to a Swedish-American girl when he worked in Minneapolis, and to this day he mournfully recalls the Sunday dinners at her home. Bob is a tireless and appreciative eater. But something happened, the sweethearts were parted. Time completed the work, and when Bob returned to Mexico he was heart whole and fancy free.

But Bob, with his sophisticated experience of boy and girl comradeship in the United States, the easy friendships, the constant "dates," was a fish out of water in Monterrey, where any exchange of pleasantries between the sexes leads either to the altar or to bullets. In Mexico,

44

life is real, life is earnest, and if you are a decent young man, its goal is a proper marriage and a large family, and the sooner the better. But Bob had no such intentions, and so he became a sort of lone wolf.

In Monterrey the ancient Spanish custom of the *serenata* exists today, in all its pristine usefulness, though it has died out in many other provincial Mexican cities. While the band plays in the center of the square, and chaperones watch from the sidelines, the girls progress around the square clockwise, while the boys walk counterclockwise. It is almost the only way young people have a chance to meet each other, unless they are invited to the same parties.

Bob used to go to the *serenatas* in Monterrey and watch the boys and girls going around the plaza, making each other occult signals, with amused contempt. He was wont to smoke a cigar and take a seat on a bench usually reserved for a chaperone and do his best to keep a straight face as the girls paraded slowly past, pretending indifference when boys wielded a fabulous eyebrow technique in their direction. He used to amuse the family by devastating imitations of these bucolic gestures, keeping us all doubled up in laughter over the dinner table. He thought the *serenatas* were a scream.

In Mexico, the sexes are separated early, and they are not allowed to fraternize, even informally, until it is time for the mating dance to begin. Girl babies are females, and they will grow up to be wives and mothers. Boys are males and are bad, wonderful, difficult to restrain and fierce, but they must be trained to grow into husbands and fathers. It is considered foolhardy to bring these essential elements of the state together before it is okay to let Nature take its course.

At four the little girls go off to catechism to the nuns,

and later to school, and the boys are sent off to the teaching brothers. The sexes are kept resolutely apart.

I digress a moment to point out that though there are public schools in Mexico, it must be remembered that ninety-five per cent of the population is staunchly Catholic. There is not a family that can scrape together the entrance fees and tuition for a Catholic school that does not do so, for both sons and daughters. If there must be a choice, the little girls are sent to the nuns. Officially, due to the anti-Catholic laws set up in the earlier part of the century, there are no nuns or teaching brothers in the whole country. But you may glimpse black-clad women in the streets sometimes, walking two by two, unpainted, modest, quiet. Who is to say that they are nuns? In Mexico people may dress as they please. And who is to say that those black-clad men hurrying through the streets are not simple citizens? If they carry prayerbooks in their hands, may not free-born Mexican citizens go to church if they wish? (There was a time, during the persecution of the Church, not so long ago, when they could not; all the more reason to defend this right now.) When doors close behind these black-clad men or women, they are safe against intrusion. No Englishman ever had a more inviolate castle than the Mexican home.

So, except for freethinkers, some country people, and the poorer classes, the majority of Mexican children are educated in private schools, usually maintained by Catholic teaching orders, often in homes given them by pious wealthy Mexicans.

Young men finish what corresponds to our high school and then prepare for their profession. Girls, on completing the regular six years of primary education, plus additional work in sewing, home-making and good manners, are sent home, ready to be married. Girls are introduced to society at the age of fifteen. The *Baile de los Quince,* or the Ball of Fifteen, is every girl's dream; her coming-out party. She may then begin to receive suitors. Naturally these suitors are much older than herself, for boys her own age are going on with their studies, being prepared for professions or commerce.

In Monterrey the *serenatas* are held in the Zaragoza Plaza on Sunday evenings, in the Purissima Plaza on Thursdays, on other evenings in the plaza of the Colegio Civil, Niño Artillero, and others. The boys and young men stroll carelessly round and round the plaza, while the girls, in little clutches of three or four, walk in the opposite direction. This brings them abreast of each other, so that looks may be exchanged.

The chaperones who load the benches on the outside edge of the square, and who seem to be knitting or indo-lently fanning themselves, never miss the twitch of a lip and are known to have ears worse than lie detectors. They keep a weather eye on the rising moon and the chimes from the church tower, so that their maidens may not stay too late.

Here in the *serenatas,* courtships begin, and the whole procedure is surrounded with such a terrifying set of rules and regulations that only the most desperately in love, the most patient, persistent, and impassioned, ever get to the altar.

When Bob had nothing better to do, he went to the *serenatas,* just for laughs.

One night, for the fun of it, he joined the boys going round and round, his cigar in his mouth, his hands in his pockets. And he came abreast of Beatriz. He has never been the same since.

Beatriz is the daughter of a doctor. She had just been graduated from the School of the Sacred Heart, and was now free to emerge into the world of men, courtship, and the *serenatas*. But she had older sisters; she was no green-horn, and she knew all the ropes.

She was everything Bob had made fun of, she was all the things he thought he didn't like. He liked small plump girls, preferably blonde, agreeable, cuddly. Beatriz is tall and willowy and haughty, in the Spanish tradition. She has night-black hair and jet-black eyes, almond shaped, the preferred *almendrados* of the gypsies. When Bob removed the cigar from his mouth and tried to get out a pleasant word, a croaked "Nice evening, isn't it?" she swept past him all disdain.

"Waddya know?" said Bob to himself. He is no fool. He knew something had happened to him. Dispiritedly he went home to ask Mamacita about all the rules and by-laws. He was floored. "No, it's too tough," he decided. "I could never go through with it all."

But somehow, he found himself at the next *serenata*. He walked morosely in line with the boys, without his cigar, without hands in his pockets. He was correctly dressed, sedate and proper. He even wore a necktie, something he seldom bothered with. Beatriz moved toward him, wear-ing a dress of palest yellow. "Who wears yellow is certain of her beauty," goes the old Spanish saying. Roberto lifted his eyebrows at her. She dropped the longest blackest lashes he had ever seen but otherwise gave no sign that he was animal, vegetable, or mineral.

He stumbled round and round the plaza, absolutely bewitched, like all the others.

I was chatting in the patio with Mamacita when he came home.

"They got me, pal," confided Roberto to me. "They waited until they saw the whites of my eyes, and then they let me have it with both barrels. I'm a dead duck."

He lurched toward his room.

"He is in love," remarked Mamacita. "*Pobrecito* (Poor thing)."

So began that memorable courtship, which I watched breathlessly. If you think that life in the provinces is dull and quiet, you ought to be on one end of a Mexican courtship, or even an innocent bystander. Nothing is more dramatic, intense and formal, with absolute doom falling on either partner who takes a step out of line or does anything not strictly according to the numerous iron-clad rules. When we finally got Beatriz and Bob to the altar he had dwindled down twenty pounds, and she, a tall girl, was a wraith.

They had definitely been through the mill.

After the first *serenata* and the first eyebrow raising, the boy has to attend every *serenata* at which his beloved is likely to appear. Bob did this, doggedly. Week after week went by without her having noticed that he was alive and he was about to give up. Then one evening, as he came abreast of her, hopeful brows elevated pleadingly, Beatriz looked him straight in the eye and said distinctly " 'Allo!"

Bob was then permitted by the rules to break out of line and walk beside her. Like well-trained troops the girls walking with her fell back two paces to the rear.

"Say," began Bob joyfully, "I didn't know you speak English!"

"Do not spik," said Beatriz, and that was all she said to him for another couple of weeks, though they walked round and round for miles. Then she began, shyly, to chatter to him in Spanish and about a month later he had what might be construed as encouragement.

"I learned to say that word in order to interest you," she confided in Spanish.

"What word?"

" 'Allo."

"Dawg nab!" crowed Bob (his favorite oath) and she repeated wonderingly, "Dok naab?"

At this point the suitor had taken an irrevocable step. He had committed himself. This walking in the *serenata*, Roberto beside Beatriz, is no mere gesture of friendship. It is the first step in the dance of courtship. Everybody notices, everybody comments. "Roberto is courting Beatriz" the word goes around. This is important. The girls have a strong and perfectly disciplined union. If, after publicly walking with Beatriz in several *serenatas*, Roberto does not in due course take the next prescribed step, all the girls write him off as a *vacillon* . . . a playboy, a flirt; "*nada serio*" (not a bit serious) . . . and he will have a very hard job indeed getting another girl to respond to his lifted brow in the *serenata*. He may have to work *months* before a single self-respecting card-carrying member of the *señorita's* union will even say good evening.

Next the swain will have to contrive introductions to some member of the girl's family, preferably a brother. If there are no brothers, then some dragon aunt. This takes some detective work and scurrying around, and commerce being in the blood stream of the male there is occasionally a passing of bills. But the formal introduction must be achieved somehow, for the young lady alone is not permitted to invite him to call.

However, long before the invitation to call has been nailed down, the lover must do certain other things. First, he must find out where his lady goes to church and to which mass. He must contrive to be seen at this mass if it kills him. (Even if she goes to five-o'clock mass, and there are stern *señoritas* who do this, in order to test their suitor's devotion.) He must be observed standing with folded arms at the back of the church, presumably possessed by pious thoughts. The girl, of course, knows that these are diluted by amorous agitation.

Thus Roberto, long a heathen and a relapsed heretic, became an ardent attendant at mass at La Purissima every Sunday morning at six.

All this has its meaning. First, the suitor gives the girl a chance. If she never speaks to him, he cannot even begin to court. Then the introduction, to make his intentions clear, and to allow the family to check on him. No hole and corner business. Last, and very important, he must indicate that he is a decent Christian young man, and no stranger to church.

Now he is permitted to accompany her home after mass, and to carry her prayer book.

In due course, he may invite her to a movie.

The *cine*, however, must be an *afternoon* movie. Mexicans well know the pernicious effects on the young of a full moon or of any moon at all. As for a dark moonless night . . . "*Que horror!*" Having been invited to an afternoon *cine*, the girl must ask permission to attend. Until she is married, no young Mexican girl of good family may do anything whatsoever outside her home without express permission from her parents.

This permission is not tossed off indiscriminately. The whole matter has to be taken up with Mamacita, who ponders the young man's family and prospects, and thinks over his record (as supplied by the underground). There is still time to cut this thing off root and branch. An invitation to an afternoon movie in a sleepy Mexican provincial town is fraught with a good deal more drama and significance than might be assumed.

But if Mamacita, after consultation with Papacito, has been prevailed upon to grant permission to go to the movie with Roberto, it is with the stipulation that Beatriz must be accompanied by a couple of sisters and possibly an aunt or a cousin. Under no circumstances is she to go alone. Unheard of. And *not* in a car. Riding in a car unless it is overflowing with other people, in broad daylight, and with several flinty-eyed adults in the group, is considered definitely dangerous, and perhaps the Mexicans have something there. Any Mexican chaperone worth her salt is capable of producing a quart bottle of gasoline from her reticule, in case of any suspicious stalling of the motor, for every trick and falsity of the male is known to these ladies, and nobody gets up early enough in the morning to get ahead of them.

After a few afternoon movies, well-spaced, it becomes known that Beatriz and Roberto are *novios*. This means they are "going steady." It is a sort of rehearsal for being official *novios* or really engaged. But in Mexico it is almost as confining a relationship as marriage.

As soon as Beatriz admits that she is Roberto's *novia*,

she is subject to his orders, to his tastes, preferences, and indications. This is customary. He may tell her not to use any rouge or lipstick, on pain of his displeasure, or he may say "Let your hair grow, I do not care for bobbed hair," or "Never let me see that red dress again, I prefer you in pale blue." The girl is bound to obey him in everything, and furthermore, she now has to ask his permission, as well as Mamacita's and Papacito's, to do anything outside her home.

The following telephone conversation is typical; I heard it myself in several homes where there were courting young men; I do not doubt that similar exchanges occurred between Beatriz and Roberto.

The young man is called to the telephone. It is his *novia*. She wants to ask permission to go to have her hair dressed.

"At what time?" asks the *novio* sternly. "Which beauty shop? Who will accompany you? Mind you go straight home afterward. I do not want you to associate with Nena Gonzalez, she has had three *novios* in the past year and is too frivolous. And do not have those side curls done; I like your hair loosely waved. Let's see, it is now four thirty. I will allow you one hour at the beauty shop and at five thirty exactly I will come to your balcony. Very well. Goodbye, *mi vida.*"

And so on. If the girl gets recalcitrant anywhere along the line, the word will go out along the underground to other young men of marriageable age that they had better not have anything to do with Beatriz. She is a Tartar, you can't get her to do anything for you. She won't obey, she is a bad risk.

Now since Roberto is a *novio* he may visit Beatriz at

her balcony whenever he wishes. Houses in the old part of
Monterrey are built flush to the street with great windows
open all the way down to the street. Inside are strong
wooden shutters that may be closed at night and outside
there are iron bars. These bars keep the lovers far enough
apart to take care of morals, though some bold ones may
kiss through the bars. (Better not let Mamacita catch
them, however.) Girls who live in the new American-type
houses with gardens, in Monterrey, often visit girl friends
who have barred windows, for otherwise, how will they
know the taste of the sweetheart's lips? Because Papacito's
preference for an American-type home will never change
his attitude about his daughter, and who can steal a kiss in the
living room with Papacito and Mamacita on the next sofa?

Now the *novio* may bring serenades to his love, hiring
groups of musicians to play the guitar, violin, and bass viol,
and he may sing with their accompaniment if he has a
good voice. Usually the serenades occur after midnight,
and the young lady may not show herself at the window
in her night dress, so the lover takes a chance that she
notices and listens. Sometimes the unfortunate girl notices
too well. One young friend of mine rang up her *novio* one
morning to thank him for the lovely *gallo* or serenade and
he answered unpleasantly, "What serenade?"

"Why, the one you brought to my window last night!"
cried my friend.

If she had been quick-witted, she might have scented
trouble and have turned aside from danger by pretending
that she was twitting him.

But my feeble-minded friend plunged on, "The musicians played 'Pity, Pity On Me Who Suffer' three times!
You know it is my favorite song."

The *novio* had not sent the *gallo*; indeed a rival had brought it to the window of his hopeless love. The *novio* suspected this, he accused the girl of flirting. She said he should have thought of serenading her at least. One word led to another, and the awful consequence was that they proceeded to *terminar*, or terminate relations.

To *terminar* means literally "to finish." This is a serious, a heart-rending business. In the provinces, the idea that you can be *novios* one day and simple friends the next is incomprehensible. No such wishy-washy relationships are allowed. You are in love or you hate each other. You are a man or a mouse. You certainly do not pretend, if you are the girl, that the louse who has caused you to terminate with him is worth even the nod of a head if you meet him on the street. He has done something horrible to you; he has caused you to lose your time. Now you have to begin all over. Of course, it is well within the bounds of possibility, that if the *novio* goes through enough humble eating of crow or if he is seen with a gun at his temple by a reliable witness, you may accept him back as a *novio* again. The point is, emotions have to be at white heat or none of it is any fun.

The actual conducting of a termination is as formal as a *pavanne*. Usually the bitter *novios* meet at the girl's balcony. All gifts are returned, in deadly silence. Especially he must give back her holy medal, which she had loaned him as a special pledge. There is perhaps one polite, or despairing, kiss on the hand. The broken-hearted *novio* slinks away into the dark while the *novia* throws herself across her bed in a storm of sobs. Or maybe the *novio* if he is a clod (there are some clods!) swaggers away whistling, acting relieved. *Infame!*

The moment comes when Roberto must take the final step. He must ask to call. Permission is granted. The date and the hour for the call are arranged. The moment the doors of the *zaguan* of Beatriz's house clang shut behind him, he is an engaged man. He is now what is called the "official" or accepted *novio*.

At each step of the courtship the *novio* must go one pace further or he stands to be blacklisted for years. And all the while he is subjected to a fanatical and constant spy system. All the friends and relatives of the girl render her regular daily reports on the *novio's* movements. Woe if he has been seen walking home from mass with some other *señorita!* Woe if he has been caught near the balcony of some rival charmer. Woe if he has made a trip out of the city without the express permission of his *novia!* Woe if he has been observed in swimming without wearing around his neck on a chain the holy medal of his sweetheart!

After he became the *novio* official, Roberto was able to invite Beatriz to an evening dance, accompanied by other *parejas* of his brother and wife, or her brothers. Naturally Beatriz danced only with Roberto and Roberto only with Beatriz. They would both be thought libidinous were they to stand and gyrate in the embrace of any other person!

On a certain day, therefore, Mamacita made Papacito put on his best suit, and she arrayed herself in her best black crepe and her formal hat with plumes. They were to accompany Roberto (nervous and muttering Dog-nab every few minutes) to the home of Beatriz to *pedir* her. To formally ask for her hand in marriage.

In the doctor's formal *sala* the four parents sat in dignified conclave. Mamacita and Papacito indicated Roberto's solvency and nobility of character. Beatriz's parents took these matters into careful consideration. Vermouth and sweet cakes went round. At last a formal date was set for the wedding. It was to be six months' distant. Beatriz needed a tonic, her doctor father thought. Roberto had to save up for the expenses of the wedding.

It is customary for the *novio* to give the *novia* a sum of money to cover the purchase of her wedding gown, slippers, veil, underclothing and flowers, and all the clothes she will need for her trousseau, as well as the traveling expenses of herself and a chaperone, while she goes to the nearest large city to buy her things. This dates from the old tradition of the Mexican gentleman bringing his bride a coffer in which are her wedding garments.

Meanwhile, he gets busy finding a house and furnishing it. Some of the trouble and expense of furnishing the home is taken care of by a canvas of possible wedding gifts. Thus maybe the girl's parents intend to give her a rug and a sofa for the *sala*, while his will give the bedroom. An uncle is touched for the stove and some kitchen furniture. A group of the *novio's* friends chip in to purchase a dining-room set. And so on. But whatever he lacks, the bridegroom must provide himself.

The maiden brings to her marriage her linens, some gifts, and her lovely self. Nothing more. The bridegroom even pays for the wedding reception and banquet.

All the girl's family is obligated to pay for, is the "civil" wedding, which, according to Mexican law, is the only one establishing legal rights. This must be performed by a judge, and duly registered. However, only a small percentage of citizens consider that this civil wedding is the real one. The real wedding takes place before the altar in church. Thus it often happens, that due to churches being booked full for weddings, and due to tradition itself which counsels a lag between the civil and the religious ceremonies, the young married woman, who has been legally united to her husband by a judge, remains in her father's home another month or so, and then is married in church. Only then may the wedding journey take place; only then are the young people really considered man and wife by all their Catholic families and feelings.

Roberto's courtship was spangled with dramatic quarrels and reconciliations. Once they terminated. Beatriz threw the book at him, as the saying goes. After all, he had been away from Monterrey a long time, and a girl can't be too careful. He might have got some of those strange foreign ideas in the United States. Several times the *novia* exercised one of her privileges, which is to impose a *castigo* or chastisement. To punish the *novio* for some offence, she tells him that she will not see him or answer his phone calls for a fixed period of time. The underground gets into action at once. He has to prove his love by phoning regularly and pleading for a word; by moping around, sending flowers, and generally demonstrating that he adores her. If he is seen at a dance or a *serenata* or even a movie, he is done for. Roberto took to his cigar.

Their wedding was charming. The old Mexican custom indicates that the couple are met by the priest at the door of the church and there married. The bridegroom passes the bride moneys of gold and silver, to indicate that he endows her with all his worldly goods. Then, when mass begins, they hear mass together as man and wife on their knees. Tall candles burn in front of them, for fertility. During the mass, the bridegroom is enveloped in the bride's veil, at one point, to show that she will protect and care for his comfort and at another point, they are bound together with a chain of flowers.

Some weeks after his marriage, when they had returned from their honeymoon, Roberto came to see us. He was a happy young bridegroom. But he had spent ten thousand pesos and the purpose of his visit was to congratulate Luis on having had the good sense to marry a foreign woman who didn't know all about these expensive customs.

"I can tell you it will take me years to save up that much money again," declared Roberto, "and you can bet I'll never get a divorce! Dog-nab!"

This was a pertinent comment on the extremely low divorce rate in Mexico, especially in the provinces, not entirely, it would seem, due to the disapproval of the Church.

Getting a wife is darned costly, and once you've got one, she simply has to do!

VIII

EXACTLY A MONTH after Luis and I had been married, my sister-in-law Adela phoned me.

"Well, any news?" she inquired eagerly.

"Why . . . why no, not especially."

"Oh, too bad." Her low voice throbbed with sympathy.

Later on Mamacita called up. She did not ask specifically for news but her voice had the effect that she expected to be told something. Reluctantly, she rang off.

That afternoon Mamacita, Tia Rosa, and Ernesto's wife Angelita came to visit me. They all looked at me intensely and asked me repeatedly how I felt.

"Why I feel wonderful!"

The three faces fell.

"Not even a little nausea in the morning . . . or anything?"

At last I tumbled.

"No, I'm fine," I explained.

A few days later I asked Luis to take me to a doctor to have my ears pierced.

According to Mexican custom I had been given some lovely sets of antique jewelry as a wedding present, and I wanted to be able to wear the earrings. As they were for pierced ears, the solution was obvious.

I waited my turn in the doctor's office, was scolded for having used screw earrings which had caused me to grow a corn inside one ear lobe, and then came home with little sterile hoops of thread through each ear and instructions to keep moving them around, until the holes healed.

No sooner had I reached home than the phone rang. It was Adela.

"Aha, you were holding out on me!"

"What do you mean?"

"Diamantina saw you coming out of the doctor's office. Want to surprise everybody, is that it?"

"No. I only went to have my ears pierced."

"What?" she screamed.

"Yes, so I can wear my beautiful coral and pearl earrings."

"Oh, Mamacita's going to be awfully disappointed."

So is everybody, I reflected bitterly. I was furious at this avid interest in intimate affairs. I wondered whether they would all want to be present at the birth if and when I finally produced an offspring. I vowed that when I did have some "news," wild horses wouldn't drag it out of me. I would swear it was only just a little tumor. I spat out these rebellious thoughts to Luis, but he laughed indulgently.

But meanwhile I learned that in Monterrey (as elsewhere in the Mexican provinces) being pregnant has all sorts of advantages never dreamed of north of the border.

For one thing, everybody is pregnant all the time. This simplifies many things for the lady in waiting. No coy fashions to "hide that bulge." You wear your stomach prominently forward with a certain arrogance. No creeping about wondering whether you look too distressingly inflated. The more inflated you are, the more you will be cherished, and loving friends may stop you right on Morelos Street to feel the baby leaping about and perhaps even listen to see if they think they can detect two heart beats.

There is a gesture which means you are expecting. With the right hand you stroke the air about two feet in front of your waistline. This is constantly employed by ladies who cannot as yet prove anything by measurements. A proud prospective father presents you to a friend, makes the gestures and points his thumb at you. You are immediately leaped on and kissed by all the envious females present.

Two months went by. Adela phoned faithfully. No news. Three. Four. Mamacita brought Luis a tonic and Adela recommended that I take corn *atole* (a sort of thin gruel) in the mornings. Five months. Six. Now I began to receive visits of condolence. Adela told me about some cases in which it was the girl's fault, because her health was bad, and in some cases, it was proved that it was the man's fault because . . . Whose fault could it be?

I took this up with my husband.

"If we never have any children and they decide it is both our faults, will we have to wear white robes and ring a bell and cry 'Unclean, unclean'?" I wanted to know. "Will we be put in jail?"

"Calm down," he advised me. "Mexico is just like every place else in one respect. That is, the baby mustn't arrive before nine months and a few minutes, at least. But if the baby arrives in nine months and a day the girl is a fine healthy specimen, a perfect wife, an exemplary Christian, a wonder. You are getting way behind."

As we swung into the eighth month I discovered that

there was going to be news to purvey to about twenty palpitating ears. I had forgotten all about being secretive; I couldn't get ready fast enough to go to see Mamacita and to make the special gesture. She was sitting in her patio under the waving ferns and climbing vines, with her work basket on her lap. Her small plump hands were putting the finishing stitches into a pink *mañanita* or bed jacket.

"Just finished. For you," she said. "When will the baby arrive? October? Yes, as I thought."

She hugged and kissed me, and sent for tea for herself, and nourishing chocolate for me.

Papacito came back from his classes at the university and wandered into the patio, with a book of mathematical problems (his favorite diversion) in his hand. Mamacita told him that the sixth grandchild was on the way.

He dropped his hand on my hair lightly, and said, "Take care of yourself, *hijita*," calling me "daughter" for the first time.

After he had gone into his study Mamacita said, "Always tell him you feel well, even if you don't, because he worries so much. But always tell me exactly what you feel, for I have had ten children and I know every step of the way."

Now I was taken into the enormous intimate club of pregnant ladies which exists all the time in Monterrey, and I was taught all the rites, passwords, and secrets.

I was made to go down all stairways backwards, clinging to a strong arm. This is a wise precaution for later, when one's bulge hides the steps and one might fall. But I had to begin this while still apparently a size fourteen. And I was fed constantly. As I increased in bulk I was forbidden to carry anything, to lean down, to stretch up, to move furniture or to walk on wet pavement. I was made to drink tea made of cornsilk for my kidneys, tea made of pecan-tree leaves to make blood and tea made of fig-tree leaves for my nerves.

One day I received an invitation to play the violin at the musical club, but having calculated that I would then be well into the seventh month, I was about to refuse. This modesty of mine was greeted with indulgent laughter and I was instructed by Mamacita not to be silly but to accept at once.

On the day of the concert she arrived, bringing a maternity corset of Adela's not in active use at the time, and she personally selected a bouffant evening dress and pried me into it. I was trundled off to the concert, fiddle case under my arm. Once there I became calm at once. For every other married woman on the program was also pregnant. It seemed to us that the *señoritas* looked absurd, such small waists, poor things. And of course only we pregnant ladies could play with real expression, for after all, we knew what Life was. We were right in the middle of it, and it was right in the middle of us.

IX

WHEN WE HAD been married about six months, Mamacita suggested a shopping trip to Laredo. I was delighted with the prospect. Thus began a pattern that was to become a part of my life from then on,—the pre-summer shopping trip and the pre-Christmas shopping trip for the buying of presents and winter clothes *al otro lado* (on the other side).

In those days Monterrey had a few stores but their stocks were limited and gauged to the purses of people who could never dream of going *al otro lado*. I could never find the kind of underclothing I was used to, and shoes made in Mexico, for the tiny, short-toed, high-arched feet of the Mexican girls, wouldn't fit my typically American foot.

Shopping trips weren't made to Laredo every day, for there were the matters of papers, permissions to cross the border, customs, duties, and other bureaucratic botherations to cope with.

Laredo was only a hundred miles away, so I was quite unprepared for the fierce flutter of preparations. This was partly because I had forgotten the traditional thrift of the *Regiomontanos* (Monterrey people). The underground quickly learned that there was an expedition to Laredo underway, and all my friends and acquaintances phoned and called. They had lists of things for me to bring them if I had room.

Mamacita stayed my hand when I began busily making out lists of things to remember to purchase for Nena G., Maria L., Concha D. etc. She herself had a list covering several pages and she warned me with dark looks that I would only be allowed a fixed number of purchases that I could pass without duty for my own personal use. Duties can mount up and become distinctly unnerving. I mustn't permit acquaintances to load me up with so many requests that I wouldn't be able to bring back anything for myself.

"Let me see those lists you have," she demanded. With a pencil held firmly in her small plump hand she began cutting out the "requests."

"They think you don't know anything about the customs or how difficult the inspectors can be," she muttered to herself. "But I am here to watch over you and I am a sly old fox who wasn't born yesterday. Five pairs of silk stockings for the Nena G. indeed! And did she give you the money for them, plus something extra for the duties? I thought not. So if the customs inspector decides to take them away from you and you cannot produce them when you get back here, how can you recover what you spent for them? You are taking all the risks then, and the Nena G. with her pesos very cosy in her pocket. No, *muchas gracias!*" And she drew a line through Nena G. with such an angry stab that she broke the lead of the pencil.

Tia Rosa, Luis's favorite aunt, had arrived in Monterrey after a long session nursing a relative through a serious illness in Linares, and asked very hopefully to be allowed to come with us. I had met her only on her brief visits between her many engagements in different towns serving her relatives in one way or another, and I loved her, so I invited her to come with us, with alacrity. She conferred with Mamacita, they wrote to relatives in Nuevo Laredo and arranged to stay with them on the Mexican side while Luis and I passed the night in a hotel in Laredo. They made lists. They got nervous and wrought up as if they were going to Europe.

By the time we started, tempers were short, Luis was in a fit of nerves, Mamacita had lost her list, and Tia Rosa was beside herself with agitation because she was afraid Mamacita's blood pressure would go too high and she would be sick on the road.

I hadn't realized the reason for all this emotion over the simple trip to Laredo. But it was a sort of running the gauntlet. Customs men were always on the watch for Monterrey smugglers. Many a fine Monterrey fortune had been made in smuggling and countless were the ladies who went regularly "to buy a few clothes for themselves," which they passed duty-free as personal articles and subsequently sold once back in Monterrey. Pocket money.

And then there were the professional *chiveras* or (literally) rag pickers, who spent their time traveling to towns on the American side of the border with empty suitcases, coming back loaded, selling off their purchases in a few days, and returning to go through the same process. The economic reasons for this black-market business were clear. A dress might sell in Monterrey for four hundred pesos. But it could be bought in the United States for the equivalent of sixty pesos. Smuggled across as personal property, it paid no duty. It could then be sold at three hundred pesos, undercutting the stores, and at a profit to the lady who had provided herself with more dresses than she intended to use.

Not all the ladies who did a bit of smuggling now and then were professional *chiveras* or even had to do it to make ends meet. With many of them it was and is a kind of adventure. And the gains one can make are not to be sniffed at. These little flurries into buying and selling are known as *haciendo la lucha* or giving it a try.

Of course I am not speaking of the perfectly legitimate smuggling that everybody does. The box of American chocolates on the seat of the car, ostentatiously opened and with one or two chocolates gone (making it undutiable). The cigarettes, with the tops torn breaking the seals, causing them to be passed as undutiable, since they could not be resold. The dress (beyond the allowed six) worn as a blouse under the tailored suit. Or the smuggled stockings.

Some years before, when her children were small, Mamacita herself had once made each of her eight outraged sons wear back a pair of silk stockings under their trousers and long black cotton stockings, while she passed her permitted six pairs herself, with big innocent eyes.

Some *chiveras* get a kind of passion for the game and try harder and harder things. Once there was a rash *chivera* who borrowed a baby (for a few hours) in order to be able to smuggle a lot of baby's things across the border. (They are allowed to pass, if accompanied by the child who is to use them.) But she was thrown into quarantine with the baby, when the health officer decided he didn't care for the look of some spots on the infant. After that *chivera* got out of quarantine, she found herself on the other end of a lawsuit for kidnaping.

Once we were stopped and made to wait for hours, while the car in front of us was completely stripped and every crack and hollow in its machinery was explored. Border officials had been tipped off that a car carrying drugs was going to pass the border that day.

But when we set out on our first shopping trip to Laredo, I knew nothing of the dangers and pitfalls and I was all bright-eyed anticipation.

Not far from Monterrey we ran into a cloudburst of terrifying proportions. Luis was ordered by Mamacita to get the car under a tree. He said No, there might be lightning and it wasn't wise. She shouted angrily and he roared back. Aunt Rosa, the peacemaker, whimpered *"Adelita, por favor! Luisito, por Dios!"* but the two Treviños tore into a quarrel that made the cloudburst seem as a summer's day. Soon the rain stopped and the sun came out. Luis apologized, Mamacita laughed, they kissed and as we rolled along, she began to sing "Júrame," with great contentment.

This was my first experience as an unwilling witness to one of the sudden, hot, and acrimonious rows that burst across the Treviño scene regularly like fireworks, full of sound and fury, signifying nothing.

In halting English, Tia Rosa, who was a Gonzalez, tried to explain.

"Not too far back, ees gypsy blood, Eleesabet. These Treviño, they don't like life weethout the excitement, no? Like the orchestra. Eef nobody heet the beeg drum, they do not like."

Crossing the border to the American side was not difficult, though both Tia Rosa and Mamacita paled and breathed hard while the American officers went through their papers. Mamacita had got away from revolutions a couple of times, and besides, both had lied about their age, as usual. But they were passed without comment.

While they set out at once on an enthusiastic tour of the shops, Luis and I arranged for a room in the hotel, and then we parted and hastened on our private business, he to get a hamburger, I an ice-cream soda.

Mamacita and Tia Rosa, with relatives on the Mexican side overnight, ate their usual fare, but Luis and I had an orgy of American food,—crisp salads, sirloin steaks, (Mexican butchers cut meat in a different way altogether and the meat is usually tough, because it is seldom aged or refrigerated, but sold the day it is killed), and southern fried chicken. (In Mexico, the little hard-working chickens are never tender enough to fry.)

Then I sallied forth with my lists.

It was pretty hard to get out of the five and ten cent store long enough to buy a dress. I had never before realized what a boon these places are, with their countless variety of small objects. We had nothing remotely resembling them in Mexico.

At last I had got together a couple of cotton dresses, underclothing, stockings, cosmetics, my favorite pills.

However, there hung over us a really severe problem.

Because there was a very high duty on automobiles (there still is) I had entered the country with my car on a tourist permit, even after my marriage, so as to avoid paying the duties for a little longer. The moment I admitted Mexican residence I would have to pay it, as I would then be entitled legally to sell it, and no car may be sold on which duty has not been paid.

Luis, who was buying our furniture on time, couldn't

pay the duty when he crossed the border on our honeymoon journey, and he begged me to consent to a little delaying action. On our very next trip across the border, he promised, we would own up, pay the duties, and everything would be okay.

Nevertheless, even on this first shopping trip, we could not yet pay the duty, and I was nervous and distracted, as he took the car across the bridge, acting as my chauffeur, showing the tourist card of one Miss Elizabeth Borton, though I should not have been uneasy. Everything went off without a hitch, and I reflected that on the *next* trip, we would be able to pay, and all would be cleared up.

But by the next time, we had heard from the Little General, and he had to be saved up for.

In fact, when we made the third trip across the border this time to lay in supplies we couldn't get in Monterrey, I was obviously burgeoning.

"Luis," I begged tearfully, "we must raise the money for the duty on the car somehow, and come in as residents. I am ashamed to enter as a 'Miss' again, looking so terribly pregnant!"

"Just one more time," pleaded Luis, who couldn't bear to borrow money from anybody. "Nobody will think you are pregnant. They will only think you are very fat, or have indigestion."

So, rather bitter and self conscious, I crossed the border this time driving myself. According to the plan Luis had hatched up, I waited for him on the other side of the bridge by the little park. Luis, a Mexican citizen, would take our purchases across the bridge on foot, pay the duties, and then meet me, recognize a friend, and accept a lift to Monterrey.

But the attendant at the bridge who had passed me with a straight face as Miss Borton (they will never remember you, Luis had said) came along with Luis, carrying his bags. He stowed the bags in the car after Luis and I had said our prearranged dialogue. Then he leaned into the car to shake hands with me.

"Have a nice trip back, Mrs. Treviño," he said, kindly, "and take care of yourself. Drop us a card when the baby is born!"

Even Luis blushed.

He borrowed some money and the next week we drove back and paid our duties.

X

TOWARD THE END of the eighth month of my pregnancy I sat in my *sala* placidly knitting and purling on a garment meant for the Little General.

Mexicans being widely known as warlike, and my family having personally followed the fortunes of some of the "outs" who had sat and brooded out their exile in Los Angeles, my prospective heir was always referred to in all our letters as the Little General.

I felt very well. In fact I was appallingly vigorous, hearty, cheerful and fond of my food. I hadn't lost a single meal.

Papacito's car drew up and he jumped out and came hurrying in, bringing with him a slight aura of worry.

"Where is Luis, *hijita?*"

He paced up and down nervously until Luis arrived. They conferred in agitated Spanish.

"What's the matter?" I asked, breaking into the low-voiced conversation.

"It's about the baby," explained Luis. "It seems that there is a law that marriages of Mexican citizens outside the Republic are not recognized as legal unless they are specially registered here with a civil judge."

"Well?"

"Well . . . I haven't registered our marriage here with a civil judge. Or with anybody."

"Heavens! You'd better make an honest woman of me soon! Look at the shape I'm in!"

"I'm going right away to find out about this."

They went away together in the car, and about an hour later Luis came back and explained to me what we must do.

"Yes, this law has been on the books, but they haven't bothered people about it much. Very few Mexicans marry outside their own country. Only lately they have begun to make a big fuss about registering the children of such marriages. You see, they . . . they . . . that is . . ."

"Luis! Do you mean to say that they would consider our baby a . . . a . . ."

"Illegitimate," he put in hastily. "Of course not. We won't allow it. But it seems that this registration of our American marriage isn't so simple. I'll have to write to get photostatic copies of our marriage license and then send it to the nearest Mexican consulate for them to testify to the legality of the signatures, and there must be affidavits that the clerk who issued the license was in fact an accredited clerk at the time, and in that court, and . . . a whole raft of papers. Then all this has to go to Mexico City with a written solicitude, and five carbon copies and . . ."

"But it will take so long!" I wailed and I began to count up on my fingers the weeks that were left. Less than four.

Papacito had a suggestion.

"Why don't you just get married again? Here. Save all that botheration."

"And time!" I burst in. "It would be awfully nice to be legally married at least a few days before the baby is born!"

So Luis went out to collect some friends to serve as witnesses, and to contract for the judge to come with his registry book and marry us the very next evening, "*por lo civil.*"

Somewhat fluttery, for one doesn't get married every day, I dressed my hair carefully and found a flowered silk dress into which I could still pour myself.

Although the most important wedding in Mexico is the religious one, nevertheless, civil weddings which precede them are lively affairs, with the popping of champagne corks, and the passing of sandwiches and cakes, and general merriment prevails.

No doubt the little judge who had been contracted to come and marry the fifth Treviño to a foreign woman had dreams of dancing and feasting in his head, behind the two looped black curls which rested on his forehead. But the house to which he was brought, with his enormous registry books, was not lighted and decorated. An elderly gentleman met him at the door and guided him silently to a seat, arranged his books on a table before him, set ink and pen close to his hand. There seemed to be no guests other than the two tall young men who were to serve as witnesses. The bridegroom was taciturn. Then Mamacita led in the very pregnant bride, and it all came clear!

The judge leaped up and offered the humiliated maiden his arm, and led me to a soft chair, ostentatiously arranging cushions around me. He then went back to preside over his books, but not before giving Luis, the seducer, the monster, a very dirty look.

"Name?" he asked me.

I told my name.

"Residence?"

I gave the address of our house. "Morelos 829, Monterrey."

The little judge paused. His brow clouded.

"Doesn't look so well," he pointed out to me softly. "That's the number of this house, the residence of your . . . shall we say? husband. Let us put down on the book another address, shall we?"

I now decided that I ought to play up to my role a little, so I wept into my handkerchief.

"But my parents . . ." I stuttered.

"They are dead?"

"No. It is . . ."

"They would not like you to use your home address?"

"No, it is all right. They have forgiven me," I sniffed. "But they live so far away . . ."

Luis looked thunderstruck, but Papacito stifled a giggle.

"I will make up a residence for you!" volunteered the judge, and he rolled his eyes upward, seeking inspiration. Then with a great flourish he wrote down in his book, "No. 100, Street of the Roses."

"Now," he continued, "your age?"

I caught Mamacita's eye on me in fierce reminder. We had had this all out about telling one's age.

"Never tell your age, Eleesabet," she had warned me, after I had innocently revealed the horrendous total of my years one time to a person who had no business knowing my guilty secrets. "Always tell at least five years less, for everybody will automatically add on five anyhow, because everybody automatically subtracts five. You understand?"

"Yes, but . . ."

"Of course, when you get near something terrible, like thirty . . . or forty . . . you simply stay at twenty-nine or thirty-nine for a reasonable period. That's natural."

"Of course. But . . ."

"And if you really look quite young, why go around giving yourself disadvantages? Besides the normal five you subtract because of the five people will automatically add, you might as well subtract a few more, just in case."

I knew that at fifteen girls made their debuts, and were known to be ready for marriage, at twenty they are definitely getting on, and at twenty-five, if still unmarried, they are old maids and there's nothing to do about it. So there was the reason for Mamacita's point of view. She didn't want the world to know that Luis had married a hag rising thirty . . . several years beyond the last permissible outpost of twenty-five.

I thought, "There are a lot of lies on this document to begin with, so what do a few more matter?" I said firmly to the judge, "My age is 22."

He wrote it down without a quiver.

He then dismissed me, arranged my cushions once more, picked up my damp handkerchief, and turned with a stern face to Luis.

"Name?"

"Luis Treviño Gómez."

"Residence?"

"Morelos 829."

When the judge came to age, I nearly fainted to hear my husband, whom I knew to be thirty-two, answer, "Twenty-six."

The witnesses also gave their personal data, probably also revising their ages downward, and after Luis and I had both signed the book, we were to all intents and purposes married.

Then, about to date the document, the little judge took a long look at my waistline, calculated swiftly, and wrote down a date some eight months previous. At this delicacy, I thought it proper to cast myself into his arms, in grateful tears. The judge patted me. Luis wrenched me from the judge's embrace, and said, "Please make a note that we were married in Bakersfield on August 10 of last year. Say that we prefer to make this marriage legal by remarriage here, rather than by registration, according to law. WE WERE MARRIED OVER A YEAR AGO!"

The judge cast me a reproachful look, but he felt better after Luis made him a present of fifty pesos, and brought him a glass of cognac. We all drank to happiness.

I was not the only lady who had learned to her consternation that she wasn't entirely legal. Various startled couples got busy getting remarried, some of them in embarrassed secrecy, others with a fine flair for the dramatic. There was one couple, the R's, who, when they learned that the bar sinister hung over their four big children, sat down and made out an enormous guest list, and arranged to be married in style.

They had a lovely house, with a broad winding stairway down to the *sala*. After the guests had assembled and the judge had arrived with his books, the bride appeared at the head of the stairs. She had altered her wedding dress, but it still had a long train; this was carried by her four-year-old daughter. The bride proceeded down the stairs, on the arm of her sixteen-year-old son, while her other two daughters, aged six and ten, strewed rose petals in their path. At the foot of the stairs waited the happy husband-to-be.

This time the bewildered little judge enjoyed a real fiesta, for there was champagne and dancing far into the night. It must have been a disconcerting year for him.

I expected the Little General to arrive on November first and when the whole day went by without a twinge, I was thrown considerably off balance. A week passed and the doctor couldn't believe his own charts. Another week. I was as late finishing the business as I had been starting it. At last on Revolution Day, November twentieth, I got down to work.

We had instructions to send word to my father by wire at once when his first grandchild was born. But in Mexico, Revolution Day is sacred; absolutely everything is closed including the telegraph office, which is allowed open only for official business and military messages. But as luck would have it, there have been several rather distinguished General Treviño's in the family.

Therefore my resourceful husband, as soon as he had counted the eyes, legs, arms, fingers and toes on the recently arrived small Treviño-Borton, rushed to the telegraph office, stormed in, and shouted, "An urgent telegram from General Treviño!"

"Is it official?" quavered the clerk.

"If it isn't sent at once, you'll be court-martialed tomorrow!" roared Luis.

He then dictated to General Borton, in Bakersfield, California, the following message:

HAVE ARRIVED TRIUMPHANTLY STOP
CITY CALM BUT JUBILANT STOP
OFFICIAL RECEPTIONS BEING PLANNED

And he had the temerity to sign it

GENERAL LUIS TREVIÑO BORTON

XI

LUIS'S THREE hundred pesos a month were eked out with *buscas*. This means, more or less, money found in the street. It referred in our case specifically, to commissions on various odd bits of business, and short-term projects that might arise. Even with the peso at a seemingly sound basis of three-sixty to one American dollar, that is not much money. In a word, we were poor. So our social life, after the first big handsome ball given for us in the Jardines de Terpsicore, under the crystal parasols, was rather thin. But we had a lot of fun.

One of my first friends was Penny, wife of the American vice-consul, who blew in one afternoon when the bride was feeling miserably homesick, and spoke to her in the authentic voice of New England. "What you need," she said firmly, "is a big bowl of clam chowder, Boston style." And she took me home and made me one. She was in and out of my life, always laughing, always kindness itself, and I came to depend on her, as everybody did.

Indeed it was she who persuaded me to bathe the little General. I was afraid to. I was afraid he might slip and hit the tiled floor. I just sort of swabbed at him and powdered him, and hoped for the best. Penny took him and dunked him, saying to me,

"There's one thing you'll have to realize, right away. Babies are practically indestructible."

And then there was Camille. She was the wife of Luis' best friend, whose name also was Luis and therefore, according to Mexican custom, they called each other *Tocayo* or "Namesake." Thinking that this was a term of affection, I mistakenly called Camille *Tocaya* (to be able to call her *Tocaya* legally, she would have had to be named Eleesabet also!) but this "fell well" *cayó bien*, and we kept it up. The four of us called each other *Tocayo* and *Tocaya* indiscriminately, and the custom had the advantage that everybody else around us was thrown into utter confusion.

I met Camille and Luis one evening when arrayed in my bridal splendor (taken up, made over and dyed rose), we went to a dance at the Casino. The Casino is a sort of club consisting of the best families, and maintained by club dues from members, which keep up the dancing salon, billiards salon, restaurant, etc. Later on, we were in such financial straits that we couldn't pay our dues, but while we were paid up, we went often and danced madly and ate sparingly on the roof top. Sitting near the balcony I saw a small girl with enormous brown eyes and dark auburn hair, in a bright dress. It was Camille, and she was in her bridal garments, taken up, made over, and dyed green.

Beside her was an attentive young man with sandy hair, gray-blue eyes, and an unmistakenly French appearance. I learned later that the Tocayo's family were French, though they had lived in Mexico for generations, and had intermarried with Mexicans. Yet the French stamp was on every one of them. Luis and Tocayo gave great glad shouts and fell on each other's necks. They embraced, they patted each other on the back, and shouted "*Hombre!*" Later on, they came to enough to recollect that they were married and to introduce their wives.

We had been married at about the same time, and it turned out that we lived but two blocks from each other. Their house was on Matamoros Street. We were equally poverty-stricken. So our bridge games and suppers became the backlog of our social life.

When the Tocayos came to see us, we ate in great ceremony on the small breakfast set we were buying in installments at ruinous interest. This sat in the vast windy expanse of our enormous dining room, like a bridge table in the middle of a ballroom. The Tocayo ate my exotic food (Boston baked beans and brown bread) with many authentic Gallic kisses wafted toward the ceiling from his fingertips.

Tocaya and I got it out of our spouses that the two of them had decided, when they were pals in their teens, to go away and become *frailes* (monks) together. My Luis had been detoured from this ambition by a certain black-eyed Julia, for whom he used to compose music on the piano. But Camille's Luis had indeed entered a monastery as a novice, and had liked everything about the life except that he didn't get enough to eat. When he could stand the austerity of the board no longer, he emerged into the world again. Some years later Camille came into his life like a vision. It was a great love and Camille defied every-one and everything to marry her Luis.

She had been ill for many years and had been pampered and adored by her wealthy father. He brought her to Monterrey where he thought the climate would be better for her than the hot dampness of the coast and he took a luxurious suite for her in the hotel where Toyaco was a second assistant clerk. When he saw that Luis was head over heels in love with his delicate little beauty he roared like the papa in a melodrama, and forbade Luis to draw near her again.

But Camille, who had not walked for years, was growing better and was at last able to get about a little with a cane. She had plenty of her own father's independence, and despite his orders (which she well knew were dictated out of deep affection for her and preoccupation for her health) she secretly bought thread and began to knit the fine white lace which was to be her wedding dress. The day the dress was ready, the day she took her first steps alone, she and Tocayo eloped.

Her father, who must have read a lot of Victorian novels, cut her off and sent word that he would never speak to her or receive her again. Luis took his bride home to his two bare little rooms on Matamoros Street, and the invalid girl learned to cook, to wash, to market and to manage, for they could not even afford a servant at twenty pesos a month.

They loved each other deeply and to date have nine handsome children, and Camille is strong and well and more beautiful than ever. This is a true story. I am happy to add that before he died, her father had called her to him and given her his blessing, and had asked for the love he had denied himself for years, out of wounded pride. Camille being what she is, he received that affection in generous measure, pressed down and running over.

When we went to Tocayos' to play bridge, we had to wait for Tocayo to get his wash on the line, for he had passed a law that if Camille did her clothes and his, he would do the baby's.

In cold weather we heated the room where we were to play bridge by the simple expedient of turning on the gas in the oven and lighting it. But as the Tocayos had no stove, we lit the gas from the open gas jet. It boomed out into the room with a roar, heating the place up like a furnace, while we all stood out of harm's way. Then Tocayo would turn it off, we would all rush to the table and grab our cards and bid and try to finish the hand before it got cold again. This gave us all nerves and affected our playing.

My Luis plays bridge the way he does chess, taking half an hour, if need be, to think out what would happen if he played the deuce, and what the others would then play, and what would happen next and so on. This makes him an irritating player, as he sits and rolls his eyes and mutters to himself. Eventually we would all turn on him and scold him and in great defiance he would then play the first card he could pull out of his hand. When defeated (he was always defeated) he would shout, "There! I knew that would happen! You never give me time to *think!*"

Camille's Luis usually held strange and, he thought, fascinating hands, that he was determined to have played. Only he did not want to play them himself. He was always my partner, and Camille was my Luis's partner (this was our plan in order to avoid family strife and harsh words), so Tocayo would sit silently, watching me like a hawk, until I innocently bid one something. It didn't matter what. He would then seize the bidding and hang onto it until we were up to seven something. Doubled and redoubled. Of course I was always defeated.

This went on night after night. It's a good thing we were much too poor to think of playing for money, for somebody was always set to the thousands of millions.

In the midst of our enormous scores we would all lay down our hands and begin dreamily to talk. Often with a glass of tequila near by. This is a strong, very cheap drink.

"Do you remember when we were all in San Antonio?" my Luis would begin, and Tocayo's eyes would shine with recollection, and Tocaya and I would listen and learn of their pasts.

"Once Tocayo wanted to go to the dance, and he invited an American girl," began my Luis, pointing to Camille's Luis. "Only he didn't know any English. At least not more than two or three words. When he arrived at the girl's house, the little sister came down stairs to explain that he would have to wait because the electricity had been cut off and big sister hadn't been able to curl her hair. Tocayo didn't know what all this meant. He only knew there was a hitch. Pointing at the little sister, he put his face close to hers and shouted, 'Go? Or no go?' He scared her into fits and the big sister rushed downstairs and sent him away and he never got to the dance at all."

At this revelation of his gaucherie Tocayo would be cast down and hang his head. But then he would revive, recalling some dreadful anecdote about my Luis, which he would recount with all its dramatic import.

And then there was Federico, who had closed a career as a singer in light opera and musical comedy to come home to Monterrey to struggle to make a living giving classes and organizing radio concerts because the "Nena," his wife, wanted a regular home for her babies. They had two small daughters and were expecting a third child. When this baby was born, Luis rushed over at once with the burning question. A boy?

"*Otra vieja!*" sobbed Federico. "Another hag."

He found a little house that had a small patch of patio, just enough for a few rosebushes, but he was oppressed by the future and the need of feeding his little family, and he planted corn there.

"It's a Mexican instinct, Eleesabet," he told me. "When in fear of want, plant a few seeds of corn."

His corn came up, tall and beautiful, and burgeoned with ears, but by then he was doing well on the radio and was making a good living. All the wonderful costumes from his years on the stage he portioned out for masquerades, whenever there was a party, and he himself used to delight in dressing up as the Mad Monk, and scaring all the ladies with his terrible make-up. He enjoyed these parties like a child, and he made our life happy with his Bohemian delight in all life's little quirks.

There were the kind ladies of the American colony, who came to invite me to join their Women's Club, and best of all, there was Grandma Mac.

This wonderful old lady had lived for many years in Mexico, and had loved the country well. She starved through its revolutions, she inched over its new roads as they grew, she loved and mothered everybody who came anywhere within her charmed circle. She was particularly tender of young mothers, and she used to come regularly with her car and chauffeur, and gather up Camille and me, with our babies, and take us out to the country for a picnic, and tell us stories of how she had helped her husband build railways, and had gone right along with him to camp.

During the Revolution, her husband had been British consul at Saltillo, and it was Grandma Mac who almost singlehanded found food enough to keep alive the Americans and British who stayed there. She went out into the country, unarmed, and bought rabbits, chickens, whatever she could find. She had the soul and spirit of a pioneer.

Some startled citizens recalled having seen her pull the whip away from a drayman who was beating a horse she thought overloaded, and give him a good drubbing with it. Another time, she had taken the sword away from a soldier and spanked him with the flat of it, because he had left his horse all day in the broiling sun without water.

Grandma Mac's first husband had passed away and after some years she had married a second time.

"I never lacked for beaux," she told me once, "though I wasn't a pretty girl. But I had good legs and red hair, and a woman can get a long way with those."

Well into her eighties, she was still a lively and chic little figure at parties, still had warm cookies ready for any child who called at her door, still made wonderful home-made bread which she distributed in fragrant loaves to her favorite people. Darling Grandma Mac.

For a long time our little *sala* was occupied solely by the lonesome little Rosencranz piano. But at last the carpenter brought the bench we had ordered made for it, and delivered the carved cedar coffee table, which was to be the *pièce de resistance* of the room. Later we signed up to purchase a carpet (rust with a green band), a sofa (rust), and an easy chair (green). The curtains were green. I had seen an article in a woman's magazine which told how to make yourself furniture out of old packing boxes. Well, I had a lot of old packing boxes, so I enthusiastically followed directions. I stained them brown, and piled them artistically around the *sala*, forming bookshelves and tables.

We were furnished, though not in the approved provincial Mexican style. This called for a small table in the very center of the room, against which leaned at least four fancy beaded cushions, furniture, *esquinada* (which means squaring off corners), and a large statue or picture of the Sacred Heart.

But Mamacita came bearing me a gift of the Sacred Heart, a lovely image with arms extended in the attitude of "Come all thou heavy laden," and a carved cedar stand for it, which we attached to the wall. A small candle in a red glass cup burned before this image, casting a soft warm glow over the room, welcoming us into the dark house whenever we returned from any evening festivities.

Having got our *sala* furnished, nothing would do but I must give a party. Luis tried hard to head me off about this.

"Where will the people sit?" he asked me, reasonably. Our little breakfast set, which seated four people cosily, would hardly do for a dinner party.

I remembered Beacon Hill parties, and Saturday night suppers, and a time or two in Greenwich village. So I planned a buffet. I thought of people laughingly making themselves comfortable on cushions on the floor, and in the window seats.

"They won't sit," I explained. "It will be a party where you get your plate and wander around with it and talk to people, and get acquainted."

"But in Monterrey, people all know each other to begin with. And they like to sit down," persisted Luis.

"Well, this will be different!"

"They won't like it," said Luis gloomily.

"But it isn't going to try to be a Mexican supper party, with places set and servants rushing around changing plates after each course," I insisted.

"They will expect to have tables," muttered my husband.

"But they *won't* have tables," I shouted. "I go to their houses and eat things their way. Can't they do things my way for once?"

"Oh all right, if that's the way you feel about it!"

I issued invitations and received delighted acceptances. Ernesto and Angelita, Adela and Roberto, Bob and Beatriz, Mamacita and Papacito.

My little *sala* glowed with flowers. I had lighted candles. There were places to lounge about. Cushions were at hand; in the patio canvas chairs were ranged about invitingly. The breakfast-nook table, covered with a bright cloth, held the supper I had thought appropriate and had cooked and arranged myself. Jellied fish, a vegetable salad with sour cream dressing, small rolls. I planned to bring in cake and coffee later.

The family arrived, dressed to the nines, no doubt at the royal command of Mamacita who was always fiercely protective of Eleesabet and all her works. Luis, pale with misgivings, for he had said we would need more food, and I had overruled him with great arrogance, took coats and laid them in our bedroom. When all had arrived, I indicated the dainty table. Nobody seemed to know just what to do. Wives looked at husbands; husbands elevated brows questioningly toward wives.

"Oh, *snacks!*" said Bob, and the dear man took up his plate and loaded it with fish and salad. He was followed uncertainly by the others. I went happily to the kitchen to heat more rolls.

Now my house was designed so that it was a good half block to the kitchen, walking briskly along the corridor. By the time I got back to the *sala*, bearing my covered plates, all had been served. And each and every pair had somehow constructed a table.

Mamacita and Papacito were seated on the sofa, with the coffee table in front of them. Adela and Roberto had set themselves a table on the piano bench. The others had torn the packing-case bookcase apart and were dining off sections of it. All were valiantly working away.

Luis realized that the party was a flop, so he cleared his throat and said, "Now that you have had hors d'oeuvres, we are going out to dinner."

All dashed joyfully for their wraps and we went to a garden restaurant, where we were served enormous platters of roasted kid and beef ribs, stacks of tortillas, basins of chile sauce, and *casuelas* of fried beans, followed by tamales and coffee with hot milk in pint-sized mugs.

Late that night, having restored my little *sala* to order, I asked timidly, "Did it cost much?"

"Plenty," admitted my spouse sternly. "But they had a good time. Next time you want to have a party, you listen to me!"

I tried again, several times. All my parties were fiascos, for one reason or another. Outstanding was the time I had a new maid named Hilaria and had invited Adela and Roberto to supper. Adela had lived in the States and knew and liked many American dishes. But Roberto, her husband, was thoroughly Mexican, and would run a mile from anything in cream sauce.

At the time of this dinner party, my small son Luis, or Guicho as we called him, knew and used a few Spanish words. One was *basura*, the word for garbage.

The garbage-collecting system in Monterrey was as

follows: An urchin ran along the street, ahead of the
garbage wagon, ringing a bell, which warned servants to
stop what they were doing and go to the back patio to
collect the garbage and bring it out to where the refuse
wagon would pass by. There are no alleys or back doors in
Mexican homes; generally all entrances (if there are more
than one) are on the street side. So garbage must be
brought out this way. Always when I heard the warning
bell of the garbage wagon, I shouted *"Basura!"* to the
servants in the back patio, to make sure that they heard.
Guicho soon learned to take up this refrain.

Having received Hilaria into my home untrained (she
was a widow who had never worked out, she said), I
decided to train her properly, myself. The evening I had
invited Adela and Roberto to supper was her debut at
serving the table for anyone besides Luis and me. The
poor creature began to tremble with stage fright in the
morning.

She mumbled the rules to herself, over and over. First
the avocados filled with shrimp salad. Then the chicken
with rice. Put the plates down from the right, take them
away from the left. Come when the *señora* rings the little
bell, to change the plates. The coffee comes in with the
dessert. And so on. She got progressively worse during the
day, and when at last the knocker sounded, announcing
Adela and Roberto, she started and paled like a high-
school girl in her first play.

We sat down. Hilaria served the avocados correctly,
breathing loudly with concentration. Roberto shattered us
by carefully scraping the shrimp salad out of his avocado,
telling Hilaria to take it away, and to bring him some chile
serrano. He then mashed up his avocado with a fork,

mixed it with chile, and ate his own facsimile of *guacamole,* an acceptable Mexican dish. Adela glared. But Hilaria went to pieces, because this had not been rehearsed, and she didn't know what the rule was. When it was time for her to change the plates and bring in the chicken with rice, I rang my little bell, according to pre-arranged plan.

But at the bell, Guicho stood up in his crib and screamed *"Basura, basura!"*

With perfect reflexes Hilaria dropped everything in the kitchen, rushed out to the back patio and dashed past the dining room with a garbage pail on each shoulder. If she had thought, she would have remembered the signal bell and also that garbage wagons do not pass at night. But her nerves were shot. She pelted out to the front, suddenly realized her error, put the garbage pails down in the door-way, crashed back toward the kitchen, piled the rice and chicken on a platter, entered the dining room panting, placed her right foot on her left and hurtled to the floor. The platter broke, spattering rice and chicken on the guests and over the walls and floor. Hilaria burst into noisy sobs.

There was nothing to do but get our coats, step over the garbage in the doorway, and repair to the garden restaurant once more.

For a long time after this, I gave no parties, had no guests in to dinner. Once in a while I would have a single friend in for tea. I tried nothing more elaborate.

Then came the occasion of the visit of the Creole gentleman.

Among the various activities Luis undertook, was the selling of cars of lumber to the furniture factories in Monterrey. The Creole gentleman was the owner of a large lumber mill in Louisiana, and he had announced by letter that he was coming to Monterrey to choose an agent to represent his mill exclusively. Luis yearned for this appointment.

For many days prior to the visit of the man from Shreveport I was saddened to think that I seemed to be unable to do my part; I should have been able to entertain him so magnificently, set before him such delicate dishes, attend him so exquisitely, that he would approve of the husband of this wonderful wife. That's the way it happened in the magazine stories I had read.

But Luis was adamant . . . he was almost hysterical! No party, please, he begged. For the love of heaven, no party!

The gentleman from Louisiana arrived and Luis took him to visit several factories. He introduced him to the Mayor and the head of the Chamber of Commerce. He bought him beers. On the second day, at noon, he arrived home, pale with importance.

"He invites *us* to dinner," announced Luis excitedly. "You must wear your best dress. Go and have a manicure and get your hair dressed. And please darling, don't talk too much! He is a very old-fashioned gentleman and doesn't like modern women. Don't tell about the time when you were on the murder case, or when they sent you to prison to write about the bad women. . . ."

I agreed to everything humbly. I was determined to make this invitation count, to make up for the horrible dinner parties I had inflicted on Luis. I was S, S, and S. Sweet, simple, and silent. Many men have an odd phobia about women talking, I reflected; I had come across it before.

Fortunately the Creole gentleman was a kindly Frenchman with a healthy interest in his food. He said at once, "We will have a little cocktail first, shall we?"

"Delighted," agreed Luis. Behind the Frenchman's back he bent his black brows in warning at me, and mouthed in silent Spanish that I was not to order a straight tequila with lemon, but something more ladylike.

Therefore, obediently looking over the drinks and hesitating just a moment at Pink Lady, I finally decided on a Mayan Spirit. This sounded poetic, mild, and sweet. Luis and the Creole gentleman sensibly ordered dry Martinis.

Everything was very pleasant. Luis spoke authoritatively about the lumber business and about all the relatives he had who manufactured furniture, and I silently sipped my Mayan Spirit, which tasted very nice, rather like honey and licorice. The Creole gentleman masterfully ordered another round and the drinks came. Somewhere in the second drink, everything went black, as the books say, and I learned from hearsay later that I was taken home like a sack of meal in complete disgrace. I never saw the man from Louisiana again.

In the morning, as I lay on my bed of pain with an ice-bag on my head, my husband spoke to me more in sorrow than in anger.

"Now everybody in Monterrey is talking about drunken Americans again," he reported. He went on, reproachfully, "Of course I won't get the appointment. He is no doubt disgusted with . . . us. I hope your head feels a little better now. Want another aspirin? Oh well, I can get other mills. He hasn't got the only one in the United States . . ."

"Maybe I could take in washing or something," I mumbled, but the effort of speaking was like banging my head against concrete, so I gave up, and fell back moaning. At this moment the doorbell rang and Luis went to answer it.

He came back with a small package addressed to me. He helped me sit up and I opened it. It was a bottle of French perfume, appropriately titled "L'Heure Bleu," and with it was a card from the gallant Creole, reading:

"With my most sincere respects to a lady who can't drink more than one cocktail. I didn't know there were any left."

Making inquiries later Luis learned to my vindication that the Mayan Spirit was made of a particularly lethal brand of Mexican absinthe. And in due course he received a letter appointing him exclusive agent for the lumber mill in Shreveport.

XII

AS WINTER drew on in Monterrey we had a series of dramatic cloudbursts, which would come with a menacing gloom through which darted violet lightning like snake's tongues, and then a rush of water from the skies. Within a few moments our little sunken patio would be a half a foot deep in water. Soon the Santa Catarina River would come roaring down from the hills, swollen and muddy, and sometimes carrying aloft, like horrid banners, bodies of dead cows and horses that had been caught in the flood.

The Santa Catarina, usually an apologetic trickle in the middle of a wide sandy bed, becomes a monster once a year and there have been floods that made a thousand homeless and took hundreds of lives. Papacito was set in enmity against the river and had worked out a plan by which its course might be diverted behind the mountains which would then serve as a natural defense for the city. Like so many of Papacito's plans, which he developed in full with all technical considerations, it was admired but shelved during his lifetime as "too expensive." But now what is substantially his original plan is being carried out by the city. He would be glad of this and not care a fig that the final plans used carry some other name than that of Treviño.

In November I experienced my first *norte* or norther. It had been a warm muggy day and I had been sitting in my patio reading. I heard the sound of rising wind, though I could not feel it, inside our high walls. But within half an hour it was bitter cold and there was a change in the smell of the air. I went round fastening doors and shutters; out in the back patio, where the walls were lower, I saw papers sailing in the sky, tops of trees tossing in a wild dance. The door was almost wrenched from my hands by invisible giants.

"*Norte*," yelled Tomasa and she hurried into the patio to set the plants out of harm's way. As night fell the rain began. This was heavy at first and then it slowed down into a steady cold drizzle without let-up, which is known as *chipi chipi*. Policarpo, the cat, and I huddled into my fur coat and waited out the storm. But sometimes these rains lasted a week and life could lose all its rainbow colors after a week of cold and *chipi chipi*, in a walled house with stone floors, without any artificial heat whatever.

Mexicans do not like heat. Rather, they are afraid of any artificial heat, or heat not of the sun. In Monterrey in my first years as a bride, only the mad Americans had houses with fireplaces, and only quite insane people who cared nothing for their health, took the enormous risk of lighting gas heaters.

Mamacita especially had the old-fashioned Mexican idea that stoves are noxious and Luis hewed faithfully to the party line. As cold day succeeded cold day I felt more and more miserable. Luis did as he had always done. He breakfasted in his pajamas and woolly bathrobe. He lunched in his clothes and the bathrobe, and he dined in his clothes and his overcoat. This was standard practice. By spring few overcoats were not soup stained. The servant cooked in her *reboso* and several shawls. I sat around and moaned.

By December my hands were chapped from passing from cold room into cold hall in my own house and my fur coat bade fair to end the winter as decorated with spots of sauce and gravy as all the Monterrey overcoats in which business was conducted.

By day I wore a tweed skirt and twin sweaters and my fur coat. By December when I prepared for bed I put on more than I took off. Over flannel pajamas I put a sweater; I wore bed socks and various and sundry scarves and *rebosos*. I spread my fur coat, from which I couldn't bear to be parted for an instant, over my side of the bed. Policarpo purred under it all night. I woke to see my breath in the morning, I saw it at noon in my *sala* as I sat turning the collar of a shirt for Luis with stiff fingers; I could cut it into inch squares at night.

When Luis asked me what I wanted for Christmas, I was ready with my answer.

"A stove! Preferably portable!"

Mamacita explained to me that this was just asking for trouble.

"But why, Mamacita?"

"Because you will get warm."

"But I *want* to get warm!"

She explained patiently.

"If you get warm by a stove and then go into a cold room or outside, you will catch pneumonia."

"But in Boston people warm their houses and then go

out into the snowy street, and they don't *all* die of pneumonia."

"*Quien sabe* about Boston. But you are in Mexico, and *here* it is very dangerous to hover over a stove and then expose yourself to the cold."

"It's the change then, that is so dangerous?"

"Of course."

"Well, then I will promise you one thing. I will not stir from my stove except to go to bed until summer is here again."

I got my stove and I practically moved into it for the winter. Mamacita was ready for an emergency call. She kept medicine and chest plasters on her night table and she was prepared to dash and save Eleesabet from lung fever the moment the word came.

I tried in vain to explain to her that the human body can adjust to quick changes in temperature with marvelous adaptability, if they are short, but that it cannot stand prolonged discomfort. But she merely shook her head in disbelief, and pointed out that maybe that was so in my country, but in Mexico . . . she knew better.

Do not think I exaggerate the bitterness of the winter cold in "sunny Mexico." I will never forget the spectacle of a watchman whose duty it was to guard a bank on Morelos Street. He sat on a chair in front of the big entrance door to the bank wearing an overcoat, and a great shawl that wrapped round his shoulders and came up to cover his mouth and his ears. An enormous Texas Stetson hat held a little heat on his bald head. His feet were tied up in woolen scarves and he sat with them in a box, which I presume kept cold air off his ankles and protected his shoe soles from the icy sidewalk pavement. His rifle lay across his knees braced by his mittened hands.

The bank has never been assaulted but I can't think why not. Any thief should be able to break in and run away with all the money in the time it would take the watchman to unwind himself and get out of his box.

Besides the terror of heated rooms (I learned to turn off my stove whenever I had company or watch my guests huddle themselves into the farthest corner away from the heat), Mexicans attribute all sorts of dire things to artificial cold, as well. It took a long time to convince *Regiomontanos* that it wasn't better to swelter in summer than to have anything to do with air conditioning. Now there are brave souls who admit it, but with reservations.

Mamacita almost had a nervous breakdown when she learned of my suicidal devices to get cool enough to sleep in summer when the thermometer stood at over ninety day and night. By devoted prayers to our Lady of Lourdes, she had saved me from suicide with my stove during the winter. Now she had to use the same prayers but in a different key, for I took cold showers at bedtime and put on my nightgown without toweling myself, so that the silk would cling to my wet skin and keep me cool a little longer. Then I would direct the electric fan at myself, and so manage to get to sleep. Mamacita made my husband promise to turn the fan off the minute I was unconscious, and by this device, she kept life in me, she thought.

She never ceased to marvel at my bouncing good health, for I was prey to so many mortal habits, such as getting warm when I was cold, and getting cool when I was hot, and besides, I was addicted to a death-dealing practice, as well. I took *iced* drinks. When one is in perfect health, a cold drink will cause hoarseness and laryngitis, and if one goes about carelessly getting comfortable by fair means or foul, of course iced drinks will give him tonsilitis and maybe even bronchitis.

This belief is very widespread. Even Mexican doctors, who have been told it by their mothers in their youth, believe it. Children are taught to love God and go to church and never never *never* to take ice water.

Whenever there was a children's party, all the mothers, when they arrived to collect their offspring, asked, "Did you drink anything cold?" If the answer was in the affirmative, there were wails and lamentations. "Oh, now tomorrow you will have a cold on the chest, you bad boy!"

"It's curious," I said to Mamacita one day, teasing her, "that this pernicious effect of iced drinks takes place only on crossing the border. Just across, in Laredo, for instance, people drink iced pop and lemonade and nothing ever happens to them."

"Well, but we have different customs," Mamacita pointed out reasonably. "People over there are accustomed to taking cold drinks. However," she added, looking at me severely, "don't incite innocent people on this side of the border to imitate you because all Mexicans catch their death of sore throat whenever they take iced drinks!"

Night air is still under suspicion in malaria-conscious Mexico too, even though everybody knows that the bite of a certain mosquito will cause the disease. Nevertheless nobody can deny that the bad night air gave it to their grandparents, and one might as well be careful, just in case.

On emerging from theatres or homes, at night, you will

notice that even today, in provincial Mexico, prudent people cover their noses and mouths, so as not to breathe in corruption, and if they have been in a room heated by many human bodies and then come out into the night air, all the more reason to cover their faces, so as not to breathe in the lethal cold air, laden with double-barreled peril.

In general, much of the feelings of Mexicans about heat and cold in all their manifestations boils down to the ancient Spanish virtue of austerity and of accepting whatever God wills to send you in the way of weather. One should do nothing to excess, nor ever pamper the body with Lucullan comforts. There may be some mystical feeling akin to that of the evil eye in all this, for the belief in *echando ojo* or evil eye, is still strong, and has many manifestations.

My Little General had golden hair, and I formed it round my finger into dozens of ringlets. He was an angelic child—in appearance only, I hasten to say.

People used to come from across the street to lay their hands on those silken gold curls, explaining, "I saw the little angel, and I admired him. So now I must touch him, for otherwise he might fall ill of the evil eye."

I learned that if the person who had admired could be made to touch his admiration, the power of the evil eye would be broken.

Country people use various charms to keep away the evil eye, and to exorcize it. When a child sickens and dies for no reason that can be divined, it is known that some evil person put the curse of the evil eye upon him.

Making the sign of the cross will ward off any evil. That is why, when Mexicans go for a bus ride, or in airplanes, they all cross themselves before the vehicle gets under way. And painting blue bands around doorways and windows helps keep away the evil eye, for blue is the color of Our Lady.

Essentially this feeling is a fear of envy. In order not to be envied, and therefore to keep clear of the evil eye, Mexicans fall into the habit of deprecating everything they secretly love. Thus the Mexican's house is "his miserable little hovel," gifts he makes to a dear friend are a "parcel of ugly inconsequential little cast-offs," and his own children are "horrible little demons." And Mexican *señoritas* will never announce their wedding date until it is only a few days off, . . . because, they say, "it is bad luck." Thus, even in deeply Catholic Mexico, nobody will praise anything he loves too much, for the evil gods, knowing that his heart is in it, will come and take it away.

Yet, at the same time, Mexicans carry their Catholic faith into the smallest acts of every day, in a touching and beautiful way. Often, in the early morning, a vendor has begged me to buy a little something "for the cross." This means that he has as yet made no sale, and it is the custom to consecrate the first sale, that God may watch over him all the day. So, after purchasing twenty cents' worth of *aguamiel* (cane juice) or a few oranges, I would watch the seller make the sign of the cross over the sale, and say a prayer in all solemnity.

In districts where the market people have a favorite saint or temple, where they celebrate a great fiesta every year, they make a pact among themselves, to give "the cross" of every day, to the fund for fireworks and dancers. Thus one vendor may contribute a peso on Monday, ten cents Tuesday, fifteen cents Wednesday. It makes no difference what the sum may be; it was what he earned in his first sale, the one "for the cross."

Even beggars are careful of Catholic practices. Indeed, the name for beggar in Spanish is *pordiosero*, which means literally, a "For-god's-saker." This is because he asks alms for *el amor de Dios*, for the love of God. If you give alms, he will say, "May God give you more."

Certain ancient ceremonies are still part of custom in provincial Mexican families, though the original reason for their observance is entirely forgotten. One of these is "the forty days." In Mexico, certainly in the provincial Mexico I knew, no woman would ever be seen outside her house, or at any festivity, after childbirth, until she had completed the mystical "forty days." These are known as "the forty," *los cuarenta*. I asked the reason for this and was told simply that it was the custom. Probably this has come down through Catholic centuries in Spain, as a holdover from the medical lore taught Spaniards by the learned Jews of the thirteenth and fourteenth centuries. For in those times, the Jews were Europe's doctors, and in Spain the greatest of them lived and taught. The "forty days of uncleanness" is a Mosaic law, which must be completed before the woman who had given birth might take sacrifices to the temple and be "purified." In Mexico there is a river known as "La Purificacion"; it was discovered forty days after Christmas, or Nativity. This ties in with the lore so closely followed in Mexican homes after any birth.

While I was valiantly and vocally intolerant of some of the ideas expounded to me as accepted doctrine, I came round to a good many of the other "old-fashioned" dicta which at first I resisted with all the arrogance of a regular reader of the "what's new in medicine" columns.

As for the teas, the Mexican *tisanes*, I was convinced right down the line. When I am sick I now call for the special tea indicated by my symptoms and when I am well I take them as a constitutional and a general preventative. Maybe I am psycho-somatic. I only know the teas work. And besides, I like them.

Orange leaf and orange-flower tea I tried at first because I could not resist their flowery fragrance. These teas are said to calm the nerves. I can testify that they put me to sleep like a baby, no matter how bad tempered and irritable I may have been all day.

When I was anaemic, after the birth of my first child, and my red-blood corpuscle count went down to a dangerous sixty, Papacito prescribed the tea made of infusion of pecan-tree leaves, and my blood count went up to a hearty ninety. I got so full of energy they had to take it away from me.

In the maternity ward of the hospital where I produced Guicho and his small brother Enrique, recent mothers are allowed only fig-tree infusion to drink instead of water. They may take it cold or hot, with sugar and cream, or without, however they like it. It is delicious, and it "brings in the milk" for it is a mild soporific. Full of fig-tree tea, the young mothers drowse and dream, and Nature gets busy and manufactures the milk when they aren't looking and before they get into the habit of worrying about it.

Tea made of cornsilk will "clean" the kidneys and there are countless teas to settle your stomach after you have unwisely had just one more *enchilada*. Mostly these teas are delicious, and many a time Mamacita and I would secretly brew ourselves a pot of cinnamon-bark tea, or tea made of anise, or of crushed leaves of fresh mint.

Rosemary tea will darken the hair and stimulate the scalp, and tea made of the leaves of the rose of Castile (a large pink rose) will brighten and cleanse the eyes, being mildly astringent.

There is a weed called "lemon grass" which looks like reeds from which baskets might be woven, but it has a penetrating taste of lemon, and is a great stimulant.

Manzanillo flowers were sent me regularly by Mamacita, for tea made of these will turn you into a glorious blond, or settle your stomach, depending on whether you pour the tea into yourself or on your head. Mamacita was always worried for fear my hair would darken, and she depended strongly on Manzanillo flowers to keep me radiantly *güera*.

And I place great reliance on *boldo* tea, a terrible-tasting drink which preserves you from the bad after-effects of a furious quarrel with your husband. In Mexico (as in China), it is known that the liver is the cause of most of our physical woes, and that it instantly reflects any emotional trouble. If you have been caused to *hacer un coraje* which means to have a fit of temper, the wicked person who influenced you to do this serious damage to your liver is at fault, not you. And all your family and friends will rush round to boil up a good cup of *boldo,* and make you take it steaming hot, for otherwise your liver may be paralyzed for a couple of days, and you will have headaches and be laid low. Not only temper will affect your liver, but a shock, or grief, or loss. Or even a chill.

However, when it came to using home remedies on my child, I wasn't up to it. Coming home one day from a visit, I found Guicho hot and breathing fast in his crib. On his temples Blanca had pressed two little green leaves, and Tomasa had tied a red cord around his neck. This should help, but Tomasa thought maybe we had better kill a turtle and smear on a little of its blood, as well. And possibly put a fresh hen's egg under the bed, for safety. But I called the doctor!

It is hard to convince Mexicans of "new ways." Especially when they see a lot of people eventually come around to their own ways.

My books told me that I mustn't cuddle the baby, and that he must be put down to sleep in his crib, and not picked up every time he screamed. I stuck to this with self-righteous firmness, while Mamacita and Adela were practically in tears from frustration. Now the direct line from the modern Kremlin on baby care says you *must* pick them up, and whereas I held off and fed the baby every four hours, now the Party indicates a thing called "demand feeding." Mamacita knew this all the time, and the final knuckling under of the American doctors merely caused her lip to curl in scorn.

I believe that my war against the *chupon* or sugar tit, was all fought for naught, as the latest books say the babies have to suck *something,* and it might as well be a pacifier.

The *chupon* is in Mexico an old and approved custom. It is popped into the little face shortly after the baby arrives. He learns to suck, and spares the mother much trouble when put to the breast, as he has learned the muscular action needed. My son fought and screamed and struggled, and I got nervous and cried, and then my milk wouldn't come down, and they would carry him away raging with hunger. Other Mamas gave their babies pacifiers between feedings, the baby sucked and there was a little blessed peace and silence, and next time he was brought, there was probably milk for him.

And as Mamacita pointed out to me later, when the

Little General went everywhere with his thumb in his mouth, if he had been allowed a pacifier, I could now throw it away, but it was going to be a little hard to get rid of the thumb.

But I had my books on child care, in English, and I was strong minded. Until we began the unholy circus of the teething.

I hadn't slept for two nights. The baby screamed constantly, and drooled all the time, and had fever and vomited up his food. Papacito came in on one of his flying visits around to see all his grandchildren before going out to the country on an engineering job. He said, "What in the world is the matter with him?"

"He's teething," I answered mournfully.

Papacito took one look at the child's red angry face, and another at my pale, listless one, adorned by two large dark bags under the eyes. And he rushed out to his car again, coattails standing straight out behind, in his speed. I heard the car leap away. In a short time he was back, carrying a small bottle of clear liquid.

"Get me a piece of cotton," he ordered. He soaked this in the liquid, rubbed it on the baby's gums, and there was instantly a heavenly silence.

"You do this now and again and don't be afraid if a few drops slide down his throat," Papacito told me.

"What is it?"

"It's pure mescal. About ninety proof. It will numb the little gums and make him feel a pleasant glow. And *hijita*, take a little slug yourself. It will do you good."

XIII

THROUGH THE NARROW streets of any provincial Mexican town, hugging the walls, eyes downcast, hurry the women in black. Skirts to the ground, sleeves to the wrist, dresses high in the neck. Their stockings are of black cotton and they wear plain black shoes. Their faces are pale blurs, without make-up of any kind; their hair is always uncurled, dressed in a simple braided bun at the back. These are nuns, busy about their work teaching children, taking care of the sick, tending the orphans, giving classes in the catechism.

And through the same narrow streets hurry other women, very much like them in appearance, though their dresses may be of flowered cotton, and shawls of bright wool may cover their shoulders instead of black gauze mantles. These are the Mexican aunties, the unmarried women, a sort of special sisterhood, bound together in tradition and rules of self-immolation as strong as the vows which bind the nuns to their vocation.

Luis had many aunties, . . . spinsters, or widows. There were Tia Cuca, Tia Maria G, Tia Maria V, Tia Juanita, Tia Chepe, Tia Rosa. I loved Tia Rosa best of all, and as she is typical of the Mexican maiden lady and her place in life, I will tell about her.

When I met her she was of a certain age; she would never dream of telling it. She was tall and stout, with a lined, kind face, merry brown eyes, and very little gray in her brown hair, which was wadded into a tight little bun on her neck . . . that lovely curling brown hair that had caused the son of the Governor of Coahuila to ride a day on horseback in order to take a serenade to Rosita. But that had been long ago.

At once, when she met me, she clasped me and kissed me, and called me *preciosa* and *linda* and *mi vida*. I never knew anyone so prodigal of praise. She never set eyes on Luis but she commented on "the handsome small Gómez mouth," or on Jorge without pleading for a song "in your glorious voice, *Jorgito de mi alma!*" Mamacita was "Adelita, *mi amor*" and Adela, my sister-in-law, was "Nena *bonita*." Tia Rosa was so lavish in her endearments that I, used to Anglo-Saxon restraints, thought her affected, at first. But only at first.

I learned that her whole life was endless proof of her devotion. She labored unceasingly in acts of service, and she did everything with the wonderful and constant gift of her love. She was incapable of harshness. The worst I ever heard her say of anyone was a gentle *pobrecito* or "poor thing." Having criticized to that extent, she usually rushed over to the *pobrecito* with a fine cake or a pan of rolls, next day.

She adored her family, and everyone they loved.

When I arrived in Monterrey as a bride, Tia Rosa was busy in Saltillo nursing a distant member of the family—a cousin, or an aunt, or some relative by marriage—through a long and painful bout of arthritis. She did not arrive in Monterrey until some other auntie, from some other section of the family, had arrived to take over and thus release her. To release her so that she might come to Monterrey and take care of a niece through her impending confinement.

After the baby had arrived and Tia Rosa had cherished and petted and adored both the baby and the young mother and got them settled into their new life, and flattered and spoiled and waited on the young husband, she left for Linares to comfort another cousin who was going through the first dreadful days of widowhood.

Tia Rosa had no home of her own but she did not need one. She was always in demand. She was wanted everywhere. She was always being sent for. There were not enough days in the year for Tia Rosa.

When occasionally on a visit in Monterrey or some other town, she found herself with no one to nurse, no babies to be cared for, no beloved dead to be laid out, she sat down to her knitting or crocheting, or she made fantastically wonderful *marquesota* cakes, or her delicate and delicious "gypsy's arm," a kind of jelly roll with the cake slashed so that red juice runs out through the scars. How she had contrived the time I'll never know, but she had made for Luis and me, for a wedding present, a dozen doilies of the finest lace.

One day I asked her about her youth in Linares.

"Oh, it was beautiful, so happy, so lively," she cried, but without a sigh for that lovely lost time. It was a memory to treasure, that was enough. She told me about riding frisky horses through the countryside till all her hair tumbled down her back, the madcap Rosita. She danced all night in the Casino, her cheeks like carnations, and she had many suitors, for she was tall and willow slim, and a great coquette. Her dimples flashed, her teeth were white and even, her eyes a sparkling dark brown, and her feet small and high arched. There was many a serenade to Rosita, those summer nights in Linares in her youth, when the scent of the orange blossoms from the orchards hung heavy in the soft air.

"But my sisters married first, you see, and I was left alone, the last one, with Mamacita. She was a widow, so of course I could not marry. How could I go away and leave her all alone?"

This was my first introduction to the fixed Mexican custom, almost unwritten law. If the mother is a widow (and sometimes even if she is not), the last girl to marry will not do so, but will stay home, to keep her company. If the mother is an invalid, it is simply unthinkable that the last daughter in the house should leave her. Even today, even in Mexico City, this custom still persists strongly, and when broken, it is commented upon as one comments on elopements, or other inconsiderate acts, which are occasionally done, but around which there is an aura of public disapproval.

I have checked this dozens of times in my own experience. No matter how importunate the suitor, Mamacita will not be left alone. But do not think that the last girl to marry sorrows too much over her position. I have never known one who took it in bitterness that she was left with her mother. In Mexico, sacrifice is regarded as beautiful, never as deforming.

Sacrifice of personal happiness for beloved persons is performed with the whole heart, and a truly devoted love for one's parents and one's family is part of the whole social structure in Mexico, to the extent that sacrifices are gladly accepted, for the good of the family.

"The son of the Governor of Coahuila, he begged me and begged me," recalled Tia Rosa. "He was so *necio* (insistent). He was going to throw himself down from the church steeple and dear knows what all. But of course he never did. He married and now he has twelve beautiful grandchildren. God bless him, he was a handsome young fellow on his horse, straight as an arrow, though he couldn't sing on the tune at all, *pobrecito!*"

Tia Rosa in her endless journeyings, always to houses paralyzed with fear or trouble or death, or bursting at the joints with excitement of a coming wedding or birth, made every arrival a kind of small fiesta. She would descend from the bus laden with dozens of *ixtle*-fiber bags stuffed with presents.

She would put these down in the hall and run about and kiss and hug every member of the family, and then she would open the bags and take out molded pear and apple jams from Saltillo, or pulque bread or squares of home-ground chocolates; bars of candy made with milk, cane sugar, pecans, and guava, from Linares; dozens of little tray cloths stitched in her spare time; or jars of chile in vinegar; or a set of *casuelas* (clay vessels to cook in).

No matter how poor and dusty and woebegone the village from which she had just come, she had managed to find some little presents to bring forward to the next stop—a straw basket with a dozen fresh eggs, a little blessed picture from the church, or a linked string of sausages, redolent of garlic and chile.

Having cheerfully given up the possibility of marriage, Tia Rosa gave up without a qualm all the coquetries that accompany youth and courting. She loved to eat, and she grew fat, and it caused her not an instant's remorse, except when her feet grew tired in their endless errands for the family. Cosmetics she paid no attention to, except to take deep ecstatic sniffs of nice-smelling people. She did not even unbend so far as perfumed soap. "No no, *preciosa*," she would say to me, "take it away, it smells lovely, save it for the baby, *mi vida*. Bring me some good yellow laundry soap with lye in it. That's the best thing for cleaning off old hides."

Clothes? Tia Rosa adored them. For other people. She made enchanting little first communion dresses, all fine tucks of white organdy, and dancing dresses for the *baile de quince* of drifts of pink chiffon, or pale-blue silken ruffles. For herself, she sewed dresses of good stout flowered cotton, that could be washed and starched, and that were *aguantadoras*. (That is, they would stand wear.) When she was cold she wrapped herself in a black shawl and she loved bedroom slippers of warm dark felt and wore them everywhere except to church.

In only one thing—besides food—Tia Rosa indulged herself. She never missed her siesta, unless there was an emergency. Toward the end of the mid-day meal, which Tia Rosa always completed by serving herself liberally with beans fried in lard, topped with a dollop of hot chile sauce, she began to get heavy-eyed. During dessert she often ate with her head propped on her hand, to keep from nodding. Refusing coffee, she would ask to be excused, and would rise and go staggering toward a bedroom. The progress toward a bed, the lying down, were actually somnambulistic. Tia Rosa was already asleep. We would hear the squeak of the bedsprings and immediately deep snores of complete abandonment.

After sleeping exactly one hour she would awaken,

spring up, freshen herself, and come toward kitchen, sick room, or nursery with her quick step, to see what she could do to help. Then she would go to work again, as at the beginning of a day.

She was always chattering, telling anecdotes of the past, checking over news of all her far-flung family. Wonderful Mexican proverbs flowed from her lips. "Fewer burros, more corn for the rest," whenever someone rang up to advise that they couldn't make it home for lunch. "He who spits at heaven will find that it falls back on his face," when told of some person who broke religious rules. "The devil knows more mischief because he is old, than because he is the devil," whenever she heard of the foolishness of somebody old enough to know better.

One day, returning from a short journey away, I heard news that felled me like a bullet. Tia Rosa lay ill in Monterrey. She hadn't let anyone know except her sister, Tia Maria G. Tia Rosa had been operated on, and it was hoped that her disease had been conquered. It was partly modesty that had caused her to conceal the news of the operation; she exposed her body to the surgeons with a terrible sense of shame, and only because the pain had driven her to it.

I went to see her, carrying flowers, custard, lavender, cologne. She accepted the gifts sadly, and thanked me abstractedly.

As I tried to make small talk, to cheer her, to ask what I might do, she paid little attention. I stayed for half an hour and then I prepared to go. Tia Rosa, who had always been so indomitably cheerful, was crying. Gulping and sniffing like a child.

"*Ay mi vida,*" she said, "I can bear it all, the pain, the

botheration, and the nasty medicines. But oh, it is hard not to be useful any more!"

I have known many Mexican aunties who, like Tia Rosa, had been the last to marry, and then lived out their lives only to serve. Do not think she was an unusual type. The list is so long in my mind. I think of Tia Lola, Tia Josefina, Tia Lupe, Tia Leonor, Tia Concha . . . Every Mexican home has, like a guardian angel, its Tia.

Whenever I come across the Biblical words, "Behold thy handmaid," I think of Tia Rosa and all the others like her. But mostly of Tia Rosa, in her shapeless slippers and her dark cotton dress, smelling so clean and fresh of laundry soap, her face so radiant with the joys of giving.

XIV

THE LITTLE GENERAL was a beautiful baby, pink as a rose, almost without wrinkles, solemn and intelligent in appearance, with enough pale golden hair to comb into a big soft roll on the top of his head. Mamacita held him proudly and reported to all her friends and relatives that the little *gringo* was the most angelic-appearing child she had ever seen. The child, baptized Luis Federico, for his father and my father, was called Guicho for short. But Papacito always referred to him as "Mr. Borton," or "Meester," because it was evident that he was an outlander.

Having done so admirably with Guicho, I smugly awaited the appearance of my second child, certain that it would be, if anything, more amazingly beautiful. I was quickly disillusioned. Enrique (Kique, or Wicky) had thick straight black hair right down to his eyebrows, a ferocious expression on his little apple-round face, and was the color of old tomato catsup. I was a little defiant about him when Mamacita came rushing in to have a look at him. But she snatched up the little beet-red creature with a sigh of ecstasy.

"The first one is pretty," she said, "but *oh*, this one! He is gorgeous! He will have the Gómez eyes!"

The author at her first ball in the Casino of Monterrey.
The dress, made in seventeenth-century style, was of
gold brocade; the cross, mitts of black lace, and the fan
were loaned by members of the Treviño family.

Elizabeth Borton de Treviño, Mexican señora.

"Eleesabet" fondling one of her beloved cats and letting
her coffee get cold.

Ing. (which means Engineer) Porfirio Treviño Arreola, "Papacito."

Doña Adelita Gómez de Treviño, "Eleesabet's" mother-in-law, her beloved "Mamacita."

Luis Treviño-Borton, or Guicho. The Little General, at 3.

Enrique Treviño-Borton, 7 months. He has the Gómez eyes.

The family of the fifth Treviño: "Eleesabet," Kique on her lap, then Guicho, then Don Luis.

The author at the door of the little house on Morelos Street, with its barred windows. Wicky on the left, Guicho on the right.

The author and her husband, Luis—Don Luis Treviño Arreola y Gómez Sanchez de la Barquera, to give his full name.

"Eleesabet" at the market.

The author in the church garden after Mass.

The eyes weren't open; there were only two deep long creases in the small red face to indicate where eyes would be.

But Mamacita was right. When at last Wicky opened those eyes, they were enormous, velvety black, wise, and merry! The Gómez eyes.

Enrique was a Gómez, with their taste for teasing. At seven months he cracked his first joke. I was feeding him orange juice from a silver spoon, when I heard a faint metallic "clink." I thought perhaps I had dropped a pin. Another spoonful of juice. Another "clink." I looked down into the dancing Gómez eyes. Wicky was clinking a brand-new tooth against the spoon and watching me closely for my reaction. When at last I "caught on," we both laughed heartily.

I had read all the pamphlets put out by the people who know everything about everything, and I intended to bring up my child in a scientific American manner. I studied advice about how to make sure that my first son would not be jealous of the new baby. But the Little General couldn't read the pamphlets and he was as madly jealous as only a Latin can be. My life for some months consisted in preventing him from re-enacting Cain and Abel, with himself in the starring role as murderer.

Even after Enrique could walk, there was danger. Guicho had learned how to turn keys in locks. I hadn't considered that it was necessary to recount this when I left him and Enrique one day with their Aunt Maria Luisa and Mamacita, while I snatched a couple of hours for shopping. Now a water shortage had accustomed Maria Luisa to storing water in the bathtub in the afternoon, to make sure there was enough for washing in the evening.

And that day Guicho took his little brother into the bathroom, slammed and locked the door, and then spent two hours patiently trying to heave him into the tub, while his aunt and his grandmother, who could spy through the transom, raced around trying to find screwdrivers to take the door off the hinges, shouted through the transom to open the door and come out (this fell on deaf ears) and sent for the police, Luis, Papacito, and Adela, and generally went mad. Only Wicky's weight and his sturdy little legs, planted wide apart, prevented tragedy.

At last Guicho saw that fratricide would have to await a better opportunity, so he unlocked the door and strolled out, saying conversationally to his grandmother, "Hello. Anything new?"

Mamacita seized him, turned him over her knee and whacked him with a will. I came in on this scene of grand-motherly rage. Mamacita pushed the hair out of her eyes and said, "I'm sorry, Eleesabet, if your book says not to spank. Maybe it is bad for the child. But it was necessary for my blood pressure!"

After Enrique was running about, Mamacita and Adela, visiting me one day, asked, "Which is your favorite?"

I was horrified.

"Oh, I have no favorite! I love them just the same."

"Of course you love them the same. But everybody has a favorite. Which is yours?"

"I have no favorite, Mamacita."

"Kique is my favorite," she said. "He is a Gómez. He looks like my favorite brother, Loreto. But Guicho is Porfirio's favorite. He says Guicho will be a lone wolf, an independent, a revolutionary! You know Porfirio is always nonconformist."

Mamacita here referred to Papacito's lack of formal religion. He never went to mass, despite her constant prayers.

"Porfirio says," she went on, thoughtfully, "that Guicho will break all the rules. And that there is never any progress until somebody has the courage to break rules. Enrique," she concluded, "will not break rules. Enrique is a good child. He is my favorite."

Papacito's and Mamacita's selections of favorites had more to do with intuitive perception of temperament than I supposed.

Both my children have been brought up as Catholics. They were given identical training in the doctrine, and were prepared at the same time for first communion. Yet Kique, being a Gómez, like Mamacita's pious family in which there had been several nuns, reacted with fervor to the devotional teachings, had to be lifted up to kiss the hand of the image of the Virgin every night, and wore a rosary around his neck, and had one hung above his little bed. To this day, when he is in trouble, it is to his Heavenly Mother that he turns for help, though his earthly mother has all his confidence.

But Guicho has more than a drop of Papacito's nonconformist blood. After his first lessons in the doctrine, he came to ask me solemnly how the priests *knew* that the Virgin had been born and kept free of taint of sin. "Because," he said, seriously, with his fatal knowledge of himself and his tendency to judge others by Guicho, "because, what if somebody lied to them?"

When my boys were tiny I defied the Mexican custom which prescribes a *nana* to take care of each small child. This is a nursemaid whose duty it is to watch over the child from morning until night, and wait on it hand and foot. I took care of my babies myself, bathed them, dressed them, fed them, played with them. Yet my house servants were devoted to both my children and helped me with them constantly. They were always willing to rock them, sing to them, tell them stories. Here I imposed one stern rule. The babies were not to be told terrible tales of the *coco* and frightened.

The *coco* is an invention of nanas, to aid them in keeping small obstreperous children under control. He is a dreadful creature like our childhood bogey man, with an empty coconut shell for his head, and fire coming out of the holes where the eyes should be. He carries bad and disobedient children away and they are never seen again. Many a baby who awakens screaming in Mexico has been dreaming of the *coco*, for little guilt-oppressed consciences fabricate the *coco* and summon him in their dreams.

So my Hortensia and Josefina and Candelaria had to promise on the cross that they would never mention the *coco*.

I was therefore startled and confused when my two little sons blanched and ran whimpering to scuttle under their beds and hide, as the siren of the Red Cross Ambulance shrieked and the car tore past my door.

I enticed them out of hiding and asked them what they were afraid of.

"La Tu Lo-ha," they told me, with bated breath.

This is baby talk for *La Cruz Roja* or the Red Cross.

The servants, deprived of a *coco*, had told the children the Cruz Roja would get them if they didn't behave, and sure enough, there was a Tu Loja, for they had seen it and heard it, and in fact one day it shrieked up and took away the little boy from next door who must have been an awfully bad little boy indeed.

Even today I can get some good behavior by the Pavlov reflex, simply by yelling "*La Tu Loja*" when things have come to an impossible pass.

Aside from the dreadful but useful and imposing *coco*, Mexican children are controlled by a gesture most American mamas forget in kindergarten. This is the lowly pinch. In Mexico children are rarely spanked and nobody would dream of sending them to bed without supper. But Mamacita has only to arrange her fingers in the preliminary line-up for a pinch, and there is instant obedience, silence, or whatever is required.

The maternal pinch has many advantages. It is seldom fatal, it may be administered clandestinely during visits, or at church or the movies, and it is always amazingly effective. Even husbands may be kept under reasonable control in public by wifely pinches just where Mamacita used to apply them.

Besides pinching my children when it was indicated, I conditioned them to drop whatever they were holding by yelling "Put it back! Put it back!" Guicho thus chanted to himself, whenever he touched anything whatsoever, "Pitabac. Pitabac." This was his entire conversation for some time.

"Our children will be bi-lingual," I had told Luis confidently, "because the family and the servants will speak to them in Spanish, and you and I will talk to them in English."

But Time marched on and Guicho said nothing at all, except "Pitabac," "Mima" (his name for me) and "*Basura*" in either Spanish or English. One year went by, two, then three.

I frantically studied my charts of normal children, but I couldn't locate Guicho on any of them. I learned to my perturbation that if a child hadn't started to talk by the time he was three, one should begin to worry. I worried for a couple of weeks and then I dressed Guicho in his best and lugged him to the doctor.

"What is wrong with him?" I sobbed.

"Nothing. He has more sense than you have," said the doctor. "He will talk when he has something to say. You've been leaping around, anticipating everything, waiting on him. Why should he talk?

"Now you take him home and let him strictly alone for a few days and see what happens."

So I took Guicho home and forcibly prevented the servants from setting his food in front of him, blowing on it, and feeding it to him, after he had climbed up into his little high chair. The child roared with fury.

"What do you want?" I asked, and in good Spanish he answered. "I want my supper!"

Holy Remedy. He soon began to prattle with his little brother and with the cat and his toys and with visitors. He always asked ladies their age, which seems to be a good way to get a long, involved and fanciful answer. I relaxed.

He preferred Spanish to English and though I always spoke to him in English, which he understood perfectly, he invariably answered me in Spanish. The same thing happened with Enrique.

This meant that my own parents had to buy a Spanish dictionary and undertake to learn basic Spanish before the Christmas visits of their Mexican grandsons.

I recall one visit to my home when Guicho was about four. My mother and I were going out in the evening but my father didn't wish to go so he volunteered to baby sit. We left him with Guicho, already in a little sleeper suit, on his knee. He was showing the child an animal book, and on pointing out the bear, he had, after consultation with his dictionary, said clearly, "*Oso! Oso!*"

"*Oso!*" repeated Guicho.

When we reached home, my father was placidly reading in his study, a rifle at his side. All was silent.

"Good heavens, did you shoot the child?" I demanded.

"No," explained my father. "But after I sent Guicho to bed he came down crying, and explained to me that there were bears outside the window. So I got my gun, threw up the window, and said to him in faultless Spanish, 'Fear not! Grandfather will kill bear!' Whereupon I shot out into the darkness and reported the bear killed. He then cuddled down and went to sleep like a lamb."

Several nervous phone calls from neighbors convinced me that Grandfather had indeed shot the bear (with a blank, he told me).

The bear incident so endeared "*el papá de las carabinas*" to Guicho, that he christened him, not "Gramp" but "Boompa." By analogy, my mother became "Boom-ma." And so they are called by both my children, to this day.

The Mexican grandchildren were an exotic pair in the predominantly Anglo-Saxon town of my childhood. My father was somewhat perturbed about what their reception might be among children of a neighboring family from a part of Texas where Mexicans were not being treated with outstanding cordiality.

"I hope Guicho and Wicky don't get a load of discrimination at this early age," he muttered, when he saw the small fry of the Texas household turned out to play. He advised my two not to go near them but to play in their own yard. The afternoon passed without incident.

Suppers are early in my home town, and there is still an hour or so of light afterward, a great time for playing games just before bedtime.

While we were eating, the doorbell rang. My father went to answer it. On our doorstep stood the small Texan. "Can the Mexican kids come out to play?" he asked.

"They certainly can. Guicho and Wicky," he roared, "here's your chance to start a border incident!"

My two appeared at once, eager for the games. As he opened the door to let them out, my father said, "These boys are great-grandsons of General Treviño, who licked the stuffing out of some Texans not long ago. Go easy with them, for they are hot tempered."

"Okay," said Tex.

"My history may be at fault, but my psychology is effective," murmured Papa, as he curtain twitched, watching the noisy happy game of American baseball being played on our front lawn.

XV

MAMACITA and Adela were much amused by my devotion to Policarpo, my yellow tiger cat. "She'll get over this foolishness about a mere cat as soon as the baby is born," they told Luis.

But Policarpo was a comfort and a companion even after the arrival of my sons. He was extraordinarily intelligent and very affectionate. His creamy golden fur, striped with orange, was silky and short; he was slender, long-nosed and with long ears, in physical type rather like the Siamese cats. Most Mexican cats are of this conformation. The thick-furred, short-nosed cat of the Angora type is seldom seen in Mexico.

We had many games. On moonlit nights Poli would call me, in a hollow tone (this was the voice for games), and I would go out into the patio for a half hour of hide and seek. First I would hide in the recessed doorway until he had stalked me, and then dancing sideways, had slapped me on the foot with his paw. Then he in turn would run and hide behind a plant, or in a deep window ledge, until I found him and cuffed him gently. He always knew who was "it" and took turns with me scrupulously.

We played ball, with wadded balls of paper. And we

had a complicated game when I danced or practiced ballet steps, which consisted in his dashing crook-tailed between my feet while I pranced. For some reason he always growled furiously during this game.

He indicated when he was through playing games by sitting down and washing himself very ostentatiously.

I had always let Poli sit in my lap whenever he wanted to, he accompanied me at all my activities, sitting on the arm of my chair while I knitted or sewed, he listened thoughtfully when I practiced the violin or the piano.

And I carried on like a mad thing when he was stricken with the yellow vomit, inevitably fatal for cats. This is a sort of intestinal infection which begins with a frothy yellow vomit and which had killed every cat in Monterrey that caught it. Then Poli stood shivering and miserable by a little puddle of frothy yellow one morning, and I snatched him up and wrapped him in an old sweater and took him to the vet. I believe I was the first person who ever took the good man a cat to work on. He was usually busy in the country giving injections to hogs against the cholera, taking care of black leg, and doctoring horses with the heaves or the bloat. He looked at Poli and scratched his head.

"I'll fix you up some powders for him," he said. "Disinfectants. But I doubt if you can get him to take them. And he will just crawl away in a dark place and die. They all do. But here, dissolve the powder in water and do your best. Put a dish of ice water near him; he has a lot of fever."

I stopped up every possible escape to a dark little hiding place in which to crawl away and die, set the ice water by Poli, myself mixed the powders and got them down him, and I watched over him tearfully. He sat, a sad little bundle of stiff yellow fur, paws tucked under. He seemed neither to hear me come or go, and was helpless as a toy when I opened his mouth and pushed in the medicine. On the third day, when I gave the medicine, and pushed the dish of ice water nearer, he purred a little, to reassure me. On the fourth day he was better. On the sixth day he washed himself, and ate a little raw meat. Poli and I made medical history in Monterrey, where no cat ever hoped to recover from the fatal yellow vomit, and we achieved a small but permanent fame.

But Mamacita and Adela persisted in thinking that my love for my pet was a sort of deranged maternal feeling. Adela was sure of this after Guicho was born, for she would come to see me, find the baby in his crib (which was the law, according to my books) and Poli in my arms. This would almost cause her death of rage and frustration.

"Why haven't you got the baby on your lap?"

"The book says not to."

"Throw the book away."

"Oh I couldn't! It was written by the United States Government."

"Do you mean to say people don't cuddle their babies in the United States?"

"Not if they read the book."

"They are ripe for a revolution," muttered Adela darkly.

I was very self righteous about my rules, but Adela was the one with sense. For all the rules have been thrown away by now, and the scientists have learned that babies need a lot of petting in order to develop security. I consider my struggles to follow the rules—don't accustom babies to arms; don't take them up when they cry, merely see if they are all right, and let them lie there and yell; feed them on fixed schedules; constantly and firmly remove the thumb from the mouth and give no pacifiers—one of the obvious disadvantages of being literate.

Had I been ignorant I would have instinctively done all the things it now turns out were the right things to do all along. I may say in passing that when the specialists reversed themselves on baby care recently, they lost a client forever. I will never believe any specialists again, nor forgive them either.

However, even if I had not been fanatical about my government bureau book on baby care, I would never have abandoned my Poli. Mexicans though have a different attitude toward pets.

Anglo-Saxons and Americans in general tend to attribute human qualities to their pets, half in earnest, half jokingly. But Mexicans like pets because 1. They are beautiful, and 2. They are useful. A horse is a mount. A dog is a retriever or a guardian. Cats keep down mice and rats.

Poli knew he was loved and that he was beautiful, but he had his professional pride as well. Many a night was made horrible by his battles with a rat in the *caño* (an opening under the house to drain away rain water into the street). Besides listening to the screeching and snarling all night, I would have to carry away the dead rat next morning while Poli looked the other way and polished up his golden fur. He had done his part. Now he expected me to do mine.

Often in the afternoon, when he and I were alone, he would bring me some token of his esteem and his prowess,—a little silver-furred mouse, a purple and green centipede, a couple of cockroaches.

But he had his rights too, and he knew them.

In the front of the house was a little *despacho* or office, where Luis worked in the evenings. Here I made out my grocery lists and did my phoning. Poli soon learned that when I said to the butcher "And fifteen centavos' worth of meat for the cat" that he was the cat and that the meat would soon arrive.

When I sometimes teased him by not ordering, he would take me to the phone imperiously, calling to me over his shoulder and conducting me toward the *despacho*. Then he would leap up on the desk, twine himself sinuously around the phone, and almost say to me in plain words that he wanted me to order his dinner. After I did so, he would jump down, and run to the front door, where he would wait confidently for the butcher boy to arrive.

Strangest to me (and funniest) was the way in which he used to threaten me. His actions in what I am about to recount prove that he thought, that he proceeded from a fact to a premise, and from a premise to a threat.

Both my front patio and back patio were paved with big flat stones, so that I had to provide a box with soft dirt for Poli's bathroom. I bought the dirt by the sackful from a vendor whose usual cry, as he came down Morelos Street with his loaded burros, was "Loam and leaf mold for the plants!" but who, after dealing with me, also chanted, "And nice soft dirt for the kitty!" The dear little man would carry away the soiled earth, after dumping fresh soil into Poli's box and patting it down neatly.

Policarpo was a dainty fellow. He groomed his fur daily until it gleamed and he was meticulously neat about his bathroom. He didn't like the dirt to be more than three days old. When, as sometimes happened, and the dirt vendor was sick, or delayed, or just didn't come by for some reason, Poli would threaten me.

Calling to me imperiously to follow him, and holding my attention with a baleful yellow eye, he would jump up onto one of my most precious potted plants and show me just what was going to happen there if I didn't take care of the dirt in his bathroom. He never had to do more than scratch a little, and I would rush around and see that his bathroom was put in order before he was put to the necessity of shaming me completely.

When my babies were able to play with Poli, he became their favorite toy. He took an enormous amount of dragging around, and never unsheathed a claw. For years Guicho and Kique thought that Poli was the generic name for cat, and they used to call my attention to gray Poli's, and black Poli's, wherever they saw them.

But my love for my pet got the children into a long and involved difficulty with the priest who was the teacher of a class in dogma. In fact our devotion to Poli almost got us all excommunicated. Highly indignant, my two little boys came home one day to report that they were going to withdraw from the church, that they had fought with the priest, that he demanded apologies and they would not recant or repent.

It seemed that the priest had explained that animals do not have souls. Guicho and Kique took the opposite view, and could not be budged, and furthermore they said, if Poli couldn't go to heaven, they weren't interested, either.

They came to me certain that I, who loved all little furry creatures so well, and had even harbored a highly destructive squirrel named Cosme for some months, would be on their side. They wanted me to provide them with the argument that would flummox the priest for good and all on the matter of animals and their souls. There I was hoist on the horns of a dilemma. On the one side Mamacita, Tia Rosa, Luis, and all the forces of the Church, and on the other my sons and my beautiful faithful Poli. I chose for Poli and the boys.

"The proof that we have souls and can worship God is that we are made in His image, and that we are capable of love," I told the children. "Little animals are not made in His image, but they are capable of love. Ask the priest to explain that to you."

Thus I weaseled out of a frank stand and took refuge in double-talk, like my betters.

But it seemed that confronted with the question as to why animals were capable of love, sometimes of devotion unto death, the priest decided to change the subject, too, and as far as I know there has been no official pronouncement on the subject. My children, though, were convinced. Poli had a soul and would be in heaven waiting for us all, when the time came.

Like most Americans in Mexico, I was frequently upset to see the little donkeys so much overloaded and overworked. Horses too, dejected racks of bones, drag carts heavily burdened, and in the country oxen tramp round and round on a turning platform to grind maize or sugar cane. In the fields they work with their horns laced into a heavy *yugo* or yoke, in a system that has been condemned in Europe as too cruel for the beasts.

But one must remember that these animals are now the servants of a people who were for centuries their own burden bearers, and who simply have no thought of sparing anyone or anything from labor, not even themselves.

The first burros were sent out to the Indies from Spain at the request of a missionary priest whose heart bled at

seeing the natives carry heavy stones and enormous sap-
lings; he requested some work animals to lighten their
tasks. The Mexican who has a burro works him without
pity. But if he has no burro, he drives *himself* without pity.

It is not unusual in Mexico to see a man prone on the
sidewalk being loaded with a heavy piece of furniture.
After it has been laced into position with ropes and braced
with a piece of leather which passes across the man's
forehead, he is helped to his feet, and half bent in two, to
accommodate the weight, he runs through the city thus
burdened, at a little trot, calling "Golpe! Golpe!" (Look
out!) as he goes.

Once I went to a carpenter and commissioned him to
make me a cedar sideboard. He agreed to deliver it a few
months later. It was brought to me, a distance of eight
miles, by an old Mexican, on his back. As he unloaded, in
my garden, he said, "*Ay, señora,* you live a good piece out
of town!"

It is hard to judge a man who throws his little beast a
few corncobs as fodder at the end of the long day's work,
when you see that the man himself sups on a small bowl
of boiled beans and a dry tortilla, with perhaps a hot chile
to bite into, for flavor, if he is lucky.

With the exception of birds, few animals are kept as
pets, without exacting some usefulness in return from
them.

Mexicans are devoted to song birds, which "make merry
the house," and to parrots. These amusing creatures appeal
to the deep-rooted sense of the ridiculous, the sly malice,
which is part of Mexican humor. Mexicans enjoy, above all
else, observing the discomfiture of the pompous.

There are countless wonderful jokes about parrots, most

of them obscene, and a whole folklore has grown up around them.

But there was a parrot I knew, who was not obscene, and who never said bad words. He had been brought up by two pious old ladies, and every evening after his cage was covered and darkened, he recited his Rosary, five decades of it, and finished with the Lord's Prayer and a Gloria, like the good Catholic he was.

A parrot who lived across the street from me occasionally bought a load of wood, to everybody's consternation. One day, while the mistress was out, an *arriero* came by with six burros loaded with firewood.

"How much a load?" called an authoritative voice from inside Morelos 820.

"Four pesos," was the answer.

"Two and a half," quick as a flash, from inside.

"Three," from the *arriero*.

"Done," shouted the voice. "Throw down the loads."

The mistress, arriving home an hour or so later, hadn't the heart to make the *arriero* repack his beasts. She paid up, the victim of her parrot's business acumen.

XVI

DESPITE THE NEWNESS of my life, my growing affection for everyone in my Mexican family, my love for my children and Policarpo and my plants, I still had free time, and there were days when I felt a great vacancy where my music used to be. I would get out my violin and practice faithfully for some days, hearing the other parts in my head. But it was disappointing. I would wrap my fiddle in silk and lay it away in its case again.

One afternoon I went to Mamacita's house with the intention of going to Rosary with her, when, from a house on the opposite side of the street, I heard music. It was a familiar strain, being played extremely well, on the piano. The third movement of the César Franck Sonata, that meditative and passionate soul-searching in music! I located the house from which the music emanated, and knocked excitedly at the big front door.

A servant admitted me, and in a moment a pretty girl with enormous dark eyes came out into the hall. I plunged into an explanation of who I was, and said that I too played the Franck and might I go home and get my fiddle and come back and play it with her. She clapped her hands joyously and said, "*Sí, sí!*," so I rushed home and back again, and we spent the afternoon working together in great content. Afterwards, when I went to Mamacita's, I got a thorough scolding.

"Luis has been everywhere looking for you! Somebody phoned him that they saw you in the street alone carrying a violin case!"

"Yes, Mamacita," I chattered, "I heard the Franck Sonata being played at Bolivar 485, and I went and knocked. Her name is Berta. We are going to play every week. . . ."

"Yes, yes, I know Bertita. But it was most irregular. What if it had been a *man* you had heard playing the piano?"

"Why . . . why . . . would it make so much difference?" Mamacita registered desperation.

"All the difference in the world! What would people say? Your husband is much afflicted. He was told by some stranger that his wife was ranging around in the street carrying burdens. Don't you know that your husband must always go with you and carry any large packages? Otherwise people will say he is an *Indio*. He must see where you go, leave you there safely, and come back for you at a stated time. Or a servant must accompany you and wait for you and carry your violin. And you are never, under any circumstances, to make music with a man, *alone!*"

At first, preoccupied with finding fellow musicians, I did not notice the core of Mamacita's advice. The heart of it, "What will people say?" only came to me later on.

But I had had a taste of making music again, and when Berta could not continue, for some personal reason, I began to grind, or *moler* as we say in Spanish. I ground and ground until Luis at last turned up a friend who was about to leave for the States to be married and who had revealed that his bride-to-be was a professional cellist!

At this news I was beside myself with joy. A cellist! And Monterrey was full of excellent pianists! We could form a trio!

I had to wait very patiently for my cellist. At first she and her husband were still honeymooning. Then she became ill. Then there was a death in her husband's family, and they kept mourning. But at last, we met. And as we chatted, it turned out that she was from Boston, and her father was a violinist in the wonderful Boston Symphony Orchestra, to which I had been slavishly devoted for years. And she, Nella herself, and I had almost been members of the same trio for a summer hotel job,—those vacation jobs that were so much coveted and so much competed for by the conservatory students!

So we, who had studied music in Boston, found each other in Monterrey, complete with Mexican husband each!

We invited the best pianist we knew to join us, and she accepted with alacrity. She was the fabulous Esperanza, Monterrey's child prodigy, who had been a pupil of Lhevinne, but who had given up music to marry and live in her own home town. She could play anything at sight and she played everything brilliantly. Small and childish in appearance, with a round smooth pretty little face and merry gray eyes, when she sat down at a piano, she metamorphosed into a great force of Nature. Nella and I never got over admiring her.

Nella was slim and pale, with an aristocratic French-Flemish countenance, enormous respect for music, and great musicality. Esperanza had the technique, Nella the experience, and I the enthusiasm, for three!

Thus the Trio Clásico Femenino came into being. But since we worked twice or three times a week, all afternoon, during that first sweltering summer, we practiced in our slips, and called ourselves the Petticoat Trio. We began with Haydn, we attacked Mendelssohn, we didn't even spare Beethoven.

What lovely afternoons those were as we worked to blend ourselves into a musical entity. I had to study daily and diligently, to improve my technique, especially the bowing. Nella had to fight the heat of summer which sapped her strength and wilted her. Esperanza had to tone down her brilliant soloist technique and adapt herself to ours.

As the word went round that the two American brides were making music with Esperanza, we found ourselves besought by many other kinds and types of small chamber music groups which had been thriving in the shadows, so to speak. It is a kind of underground; when it is clear that you are one of the brethren, behold, they are to be found on every hand.

To our trio, we added a seventy-year-old German viola player, who had come out to Mexico fifty years before to die of tuberculosis. But he got over his disease, and to this day regularly beats all the young athletes at tennis. He was very shy, and used to get so distracted whenever he made a mistake, and would take up so much time stuttering and apologizing, that Nella worked out a system whereby she gave him a smart crack with her bow if he were wrong. He would agree shaking his head vigorously. Then Nella would call out the letter or the number in the music where we were to begin again, and we would all count a preliminary measure in dead seriousness, with bows, heads, or toe-tips, and . . . off again!

There was sometimes a new violin, too, a Mexican

from the capital. When he came, I was demoted to second violin. Besides playing quintets with this group, we often played string quartets with a frail gentleman who was paralyzed from the waist downward and who used to arrive in a car with a special little chair, into which his chauffeur would help him. But he could play any instrument that happened to be lacking, and always brought a selection with him, should they be needed . . . cello, violin, viola, oboe.

From among these players we got together a group to study the Schumann Quintet and we so aroused the enthusiasm of Papacito that he secretly got out the violin with which he had wooed Mamacita, had it strung up and put in order, and practiced furtively. Now and then he would rush over to my house, and play duos with me.

This was all very pleasant and well looked upon. The groups met in my home. Esperanza and Nella were deposited and collected by their respective husbands. When gentlemen played with us, husbands were always present.

But when we were asked to give a concert professionally the house came down around our ears. All three husbands had fits, augmented and made vocal by their respective mamas. To play music in your own home is one thing, everybody has his own peculiarities. But to go out on a stage and play for money is another kettle of fish!

We ladies, in danger of having our artistic souls blighted, consulted among ourselves.

"It's just as well not to accept anything in the way of engagements yet," pointed out sensible Nella. "Let us polish up a lot more. I think basically they are afraid that we might disgrace ourselves."

"Oh no," said Esperanza. "It is that the husbands do not want us to be *paid* for anything. They are afraid people will think that they don't give us enough money."

"Maybe they don't," I muttered under my breath, for I was in the middle of the Battle of the Gasto.

"Well, it isn't what *really* happens," explained Esperanza. "It is what people will say."

I had been getting lessons in this social problem for some months. "*Que van a decir la gente?*" (What will people say?) was the question that served as guide to conduct, morals, and happiness.

With Adela, this thought was sufficient to control her in any situation, to adjust her every act. She had a positive terror of being criticized. She suffered for me, because it seldom entered my head to wonder what people would say, and I charged impetuously forward with all sorts of independent and heedless acts. It was only when I saw that Mamacita and Adela were upset for me that I stopped to consider public opinion.

Papacito came to my rescue.

We were at dinner in Mamacita's house. The concert "engagement" was still pending, and was being discussed pro and con. Mamacita indicated that she was still doubtful about what people would say. Adela was sure people would say perfectly dreadful things.

"Well, if people buy tickets and pay to get in, what difference does it make what they say?" asked Papacito, feeding a morsel of chicken to Galatea, his cat, who sat by the side of his chair.

This thought struck Adela silent like a blow on the head. There was latent approval in the purchasing of a ticket. The logic of this laid her low, and with her conversion to the idea of a public appearance, all other opposition died down.

Esperanza reminded her husband that when he had courted her he had promised to let her accept engagements if they were good enough, and she showed him the chapter and verse in an early love letter, in which he had been so rash as to offer this inducement to matrimony.

As for Nella she quite simply bought herself four yards of navy-blue satin and sat down to sew.

"What's that, new curtains?" asked Leonardo, her husband.

"No, it's my new dress. For the concert," said Nella, and that was that.

We gave our concert. The hall was full. Lots of people had bought tickets and what they might whisper behind their fans was of little import and soon forgotten. People clapped madly. The newspapers gave us long and learned reviews. They pointed out that the two American ladies did very well, but that Esperanza . . . Esperanza, the darling of Monterrey, had returned to the concert stage again! She was a star in the crown of Monterrey, a pianist who would go down in history! Nella and I, who also loved and admired Esperanza, were very pleased with the reviews, and we returned to our practice in great content.

Our good families thought, perhaps reasonably, that this ought to satisfy us, but we were like kittens after their first taste of raw meat. Nothing could hold us now. We accepted a radio engagement. Our husbands accompanied us to the radio station, listened respectfully, and brought us home again. Then Nella was asked to lead the cello section, and I to be concertmaster, of an orchestra which was to play at an official function. We were to be paid well for this, union rates for three rehearsals, and extra for the performance.

I practiced mightily, for I had several difficult solo sections to play. I began to plan my life, for it seemed to me that I was happily launched on a semi-professional musical career. The day of the concert dawned and I hadn't broken my arm. I played acceptably. I fluffed no entrances, I did not chew up my solos. Nothing terrible happened. No string broke in the middle of the overture, nobody dropped his instrument, nobody's music blew away. The applause was terrific.

I was therefore unprepared for the long faces of the Treviños who were gathered at my house for cake and coffee after the concert.

"You played very well, *hijita*," said Papacito gloomily.

"The music was beautiful," sighed Mamacita. Silence. A sad silence.

"Whatever is the matter?" I demanded. "You all look as if the police would be here for me any minute."

Luis struck his brow with the flat of his hand.

"Your dress was too short!" he announced, breathing hard.

"And you sitting up there so high on the stage, to make it worse," put in Adela. "I could see your knees!"

Then came the clincher. My husband, so proud of his years in the States, so heartily "American" whenever he got a chance, so deprecatory about the old-fashioned Mexican ways, shouted,

"What will people *say?*"

I accepted no more public engagements.

But our Petticoat Trio continued to study, and those afternoons in my little *sala,* Guicho in his carriage near by, are dear memories. The delight of exploring ensemble literature, the joy of feeling ourselves improve. And the excitement of Beethoven, Brahms, Schubert! Dear gentle serious Nella . . . adorably friendly and lively Esperanza. . . .

XVII

ONE DAY a Mexican girl who had lived many years in the United States came to visit me, and after we had had tea, and had talked of various mutual friends, she said, "Aren't you bored to tears in this rancho? Come now, don't you honestly wish you lived somewhere else?"

I took time to think things over and to answer the truth.

"No," I told her. "I love the return to the past that I have found here in Mexican life. I am going backward in time, and it suits me."

"Oh you can't mean it!" she burst out, for she was unhappy in Monterrey and longed to go back to the country where she had learned what a large degree of personal freedom can mean to a woman.

I tried to explain. "My mother used to sing a song," I told her, "that said, 'Backward, turn backward, O Time, in thy flight' . . . Well, here it has happened. I am living the kind of life my grandmother used to tell about in her stories that began, 'When I was a little girl . . .' Here in the provinces, Mexicans are living in the nineteenth century. And I find I like it."

"Yes, it is Victorian."

"Not exactly. A Mexican idea of Victorian, maybe."

"But women are treated like children here, today, just as they were a century ago! I for one can't stand it."

"Yes, there is over-protection. But it has its charms. And treating Mexican women like children, for some strange reason, doesn't make them childish. Take Mamacita, for instance. She is as strong as a fortress. Nor does this treatment, this over-protection, seem to make them selfish. So many of them seem capable of enormous sacrifices for their families. And they are so devoted to their homes."

"Well, they have nothing else to think of. They are not permitted to think of anything else. Their whole life is centered on family. And they are brought up to believe that men are superior creatures; this is what galls me. Though it makes the men very happy, naturally."

"Yes. Well, happy husbands make firm marriages."

"But Mexican men are so spoiled! Haven't you noticed that everyone congratulates you that your children were boys? Haven't you heard people sympathize with the wretch who has only daughters?"

"Yes, I have. But it's still a man's world, in many ways. And I have never heard a single Mexican woman say, despite the drawbacks of her position, that she wished she were a man."

"No, that's true. We are incorrigibly feminine."

She looked miserable about this, such a pretty girl with the typically Mexican figure, round-bosomed, small-waisted, full-hipped.

"Of course you are, and I think it's wonderful! It's your power!"

After she left, I reflected at length about the Mexican women I had come to know, in their homes, in their lives, in their secret hearts. I could not change my mind about anything I had said, in any particular.

They do very little reading. Few belong to clubs where other people give them "book reviews." They seldom bother to scan the paper. Once during World War II when I said something about "the war," one of my sisters-in-law looked up from her mending to ask "What war?"

Nevertheless, they live in worlds full of danger, service, and excitement. They live in microcosm, rather than macrocosm, and in their own home and town, rather than in the world. But the battle between life and death is joined here too, and Mexican women are wholly on the side of life.

They are sorry if someone tells them that children are starving in Timbuktu, but they are so busy taking food to the families by the river bank who were flooded out of their homes, sewing layettes for the cook's daughter who has made a misstep and awaits the consequences, waiting on old Tio Arnulfo who hasn't been quite right in the head for years, *pobrecito,* that they cannot be organized to do anything for Timbuktu. Later perhaps, when they are not so busy. . . .

Indeed, the Mexican woman, despite her many servants, never needs anyone to show her what to do with her spare time. She seldom has any. In the provinces, families are very large; ten and twelve children are not uncommon. There is always another little boy or girl to coach in the catechism, or to teach his letters, and to be helped with his arithmetic; there are sweaters to be knitted, middle-sized pants to be made over into smaller pants, socks darned, shirts patched; little fingers to be guided in the correct position at the piano.

Young people are not released to their own devices, either. Girls are presided over carefully until they are safely married. Mamacita is at every ball, at most of the large parties. She is consulted about every engagement. She must give formal permission for any activity outside the home. If some Mexican young woman defies her mother and shrieks in despair, "You treat me as if I were a child!" it is not the mother who trembles and gives in. No, Mamacita answers firmly, "You *are* a child. And I command in this house." And that is that.

It is a very old custom, but still much used in provincial Mexico, that all children come to say Goodnight to their parents before retiring. All kneel to receive their mother's kiss on the brow, and her blessing; she makes the sign of the cross over each bended head, and her prayers go with them for a safe night and an untroubled awakening. Each child kisses his father's hand, and extends a round cheek for the father's tweak, pat, or kiss.

I have seen this constantly, and it never fails to move me, in its old-fashioned simplicity and faith.

By the time the oldest children are married, and the youngest children have begun to go away to school, the grandchildren appear. The circle of life continues as before.

And while Mexican homes are full of servants, they are not machines who do what they are set to do in unfailing efficiency. Many servants must be told every day what to do, or they forget. They must be watched over and cured, and nursed at times; when they marry, the lady of the house usually arranges the wedding.

And if the *señora* has no young people in her home, to watch over and instruct, and her servants are reliable and intelligent, the chances are that she has old people to care for, relatives of her own, or her husband's.

To me one of the sweetest qualities of the Mexican family is the devotion to the old. Absolutely nothing is more loved, petted, cuddled and made much of—after the baby—than the *viejita* or *viejito* of the household.

There are, in the big cities, a few "old men's homes" and "old ladies' homes." These are for the few old souls who have outlived their families, who are abandoned, who have been washed up on a lonely shore. The state takes care of them. And there are many religious societies, like the St. Vincent de Paul Society, which care for old persons who have a little income, but not enough. They are helped to live as they prefer by the ladies of the group, provided with clothes, food, medicine, or whatever they need that they cannot pay for themselves. But as a general rule, each family takes care of its own.

Countless are the Mexican homes to which I have made visits,—for tea, or to accompany the family in mourning, or to celebrate a confirmation, or a wedding, or a *despedida* (farewell) for someone going away—in which I have found, pridefully displayed like an heirloom, like a jewel in a case, an old lady or gentleman upward in the eighties, carefully dressed, perfumed and coifed. They are given the best chair, the best view of everything, the first refreshments, the affection and deference of everyone present. This is Grandfather or Grandmother, Great-aunt, or Great-uncle, or perhaps just somebody's godmother or godfather. It is unheard of that any old person who has any connection whatsoever with the family should be left alone, sad and bewildered, when the shadows of life are descending.

The idea that each young family must be free and alone, that it is their right, that they can scarcely be expected to make a go of marriage otherwise . . . does not prevail in Mexico. Whenever possible, the young married couple lives as near the girl's mother as possible. Across the street, next door, a few blocks away, or in apartments in the mother's house. If the girl's mother is dead, they live with or near the husband's mother. When time takes its toll and the mother or father of either pair is left widowed, the survivor comes to live with one of his or her children. Nobody thinks that this is a sacrifice. Maybe a little doubling up is required, but it is worth it.

Indeed, there is much to be gained by the presence of Abuelito or Abuelita in the home. Small children learn the habit of deference to their elders, for they see their parents respectfully take this attitude with Grandfather and Grandmother. There is never any problem about a baby sitter, with old persons in the home, whose diversion and joy is the grandchildren. The "baby sitter," that weird institution, is unknown in Mexico.

Even more shocking, to Mexicans, than sending one's "old ones" off to homes for the aged, would be to send them away to sanitariums, rest homes, or hospitals, when they become ill, a burdensome care, or even senile. No, this is when the *viejitos* need love and understanding, now, if ever. I never heard of a single family which did this to any old person, no matter how tiresome or how much of a responsibility.

Such a family would be ostracized; young persons would be warned not to marry into such a family which had betrayed itself as unfeeling and selfish. Suppose the old lady is bed-ridden and very querulous? Very well, her daughter will care for her and comfort her. Or her daughter-in-law. Suppose the old gentleman is irascible and pounds with his cane, or tells endless, boring stories? Very well, then he must be waited on and listened to, and soothed and petted, and made to know that he is still important to someone.

Nobody supposes that young children are injured by the presence in the home of the old, senile or even slightly demented. On the contrary, they learn that we all grow old and feeble and foolish. This is reality. And they are taught compassion and patience, both very beautiful qualities.

When there are old persons in the family, there are devotions to perform to them on fixed days, whether Abuelita or Abuelito live with this son or daughter or some other one. It happened often that I phoned a friend to invite her to tea with me, say on the following Thursday.

"Oh, I am so sorry, but Thursday is the day I visit my grandmother, who lives with my aunt Clementina. She expects me to take her to Rosary and stay for *merienda*. Could I come to tea some other day?"

The engagement to be shifted is *any other engagement*. Abuelita's day is not a movable feast.

The Mexican woman ties all her family into a unit with their special anniversaries. Besides the anniversary of the wedding of Mamacita and Papacito, there are birthdays, and saints' days. And the anniversaries of all the dear dead. On the day of San Felipe, dear Uncle Felipe is mourned, and very early the family goes to church to receive communion in his memory. They will do the same on the anniversary of Uncle Felipe's death, when they will arrange and attend a memorial mass, will later dine together, and speak often of him.

The Mexican woman lives laced into this world of family, the unending circle, the beginning and the end of life. She has security in its fullest, most spiritual sense, and that perhaps is why she is so often wise and loving. In a sad world, she lives with the feeling that sacrifice is beautiful, that service is a form of love, and that her family could not do without her.

XVIII

MEXICAN WOMEN have their favorite emotions, I learned, not always coinciding with my Anglo-Saxon admirations.

One day I rang up Adela to invite her to come to my house next day.

"Oh, I can't," Adela told me, importantly. "I'm being punished."

"Punished? For what?"

"I had permission to use Roberto's car yesterday until six, but I didn't get home until seven. He was so jealous! So he locked me in my room, and here I am."

"Well, climb out of the window! I never heard of such a thing!" I shouted, thoroughly outraged.

"Oh no," cried Adela. "I have to stay in my room three days. *Estoy castigada.* (I am being chastised.)"

But she sounded very proud and happy, as indeed she was.

When after due chastisement, Roberto let her out of durance vile, and she asked and was granted permission to come to see me, I asked what in the world she meant by this childish business of staying locked in her room.

Adela was eager to explain.

"Why I've been trying to make him jealous for *months*,"

she crowed, "and at last, when I came home so late and wouldn't say where I had been, he got really wild! It was wonderful."

I was dashed.

"But he suffered, then?"

"Terribly. It was marvelous."

"But Adela, if you love him, why do you want him to suffer?"

"Because he makes me suffer all the time. I'm furiously jealous, you know! Furiously!"

"What does he do?"

"It isn't what he does. It's just that *I don't know what he does*. That's what makes me so crazy."

"Well, good lord, he can't do much here, in this town where you were brought up together, where everybody knows everybody else and everybody knows he is married to you!"

"Once Diamantina saw him driving down Madero with a blond on the front seat with him," contributed Adela darkly.

"But, gracious woman, maybe it was I!"

"It wasn't you."

"Maybe he was giving a lift to a friend."

"No, impossible. No decent woman accepts lifts from any man in an automobile, if he is without his wife."

I was to learn that Adela was right about this.

One day the Petticoat Trio practiced until after dark, and I said to Nella and Esperanza, "Wait a little, and Luis will take you home in the car."

"Oh no!" cried Esperanza. "I couldn't be seen riding in a car with Luis. Not unless you come."

"Why not?" asked Nella innocently.

"What would people say?" responded Esperanza, and that settled it. It was clear that this simply wasn't done.

I brooded a lot about Adela and her jealousy. Then a big family scandal broke around our heads.

Bob and Beatriz were in great turmoil. Beatriz had started to arrange Bob's dresser drawers one day and she came across a glove that was not hers. A woman's glove. When Bob came home, she ran at him, snatched the cigar out of his mouth and screamed that she was leaving him, that instant! And she went home (one block) to her mother.

After the row boiled down to the fact that she had found the glove, Bob had to go to get Mamacita and take her as witness that the glove was hers, that she had left it in the car one day and that he, Bob, had forgotten to return it to her. Mamacita brought the mate of the glove, to clinch things. Then Beatriz forgave Bob; she fell on his neck weeping. He patted her and asked her to return home with him, and at last he led her back.

I talked this over with Mamacita, who hadn't been a bit surprised at any of it.

"But, Mamacita," I gasped. "It is dreadful to live this way. Don't people trust each other at all?"

"Trusting is very nice and calm," said Mamacita, taking up her crocheting, "but not half so much fun!"

"Mamacita, don't try to tell me *you* were ever so jealous!"

"I was much worse," she confided. "Once I followed Porfirio all day in a hired carriage. It cost me one hundred pesos."

"And what did you find out?"

"That he had been telling me the truth." She threw her head back and laughed heartily. "*Hija,* I experienced *all* the emotions that day in the carriage."

"But I don't want to be this way, Mamacita," I told her. "In the United States, it is true, we feel jealous at times, just like anybody else . . ."

"Not like Latins," she broke in, somewhat smug.

"But we are ashamed to show it. It seems that here the opposite is true. Even when you are just a little bit jealous, you exaggerate it!"

She leaned toward me confidentially.

"But of course, *hijita*. One must exaggerate a little. Sometimes, when Luis asks you if you love him, perhaps you do not love him very much at just that moment. Perhaps you are a little annoyed with him, perhaps he has been dull or irritating. But you exaggerate, do you not? You swear that you adore him, don't you?"

"Well, yes," I admitted.

"The home is built around duties and emotions," said Mamacita. "The duties, anybody can take care of them. The emotions, these are more delicate. One must handle them like an artist. Jealousy pleases the men very much, *hijita*. You have no idea how important it makes them feel."

"Yes, but . . ."

"Oh, I know the American girls do not like feigning; they despise using the old-fashioned trap to catch the man. But I notice that all their frankness does not help much in preserving love. Is it not so? Do not three out of five marriages end in divorce?"

"Yes, those are the figures."

"Do you know what I think?"

"Tell me."

"Is it not so, that the one who wants the divorce usually marries again?"

"It often happens."

"Then I say that it is better, instead of being so frank and trusting and allowing the wife or husband to look for excitement in a new courtship, to make such a terrible big scandal that it is more fun to court the same husband or wife back again. Like Bob and Beatriz. Bob has had such a crisis in the nerves, such a drama, such a difficulty about this glove, that Beatriz will have no fears that he may seek excitement anywhere else for at least two years."

"Well, I see what you mean. What the Greeks used to call 'a purging of the emotions.'"

"Yes. I think it is healthy. That is why I hid my glove in Roberto's bureau drawer."

"Mamacita! You didn't!"

"I did. And all has happened as I planned. I am very pleased."

"You are as bad as Adela!"

"No, no. It is better to prevent than to cry, don't you have this saying in English? Well, you know Roberto must go soon to the United States on a long business trip, and Beatriz cannot accompany him because she is in a delicate condition. I arrange that she shall not worry."

"I don't understand."

"Maybe not. You say that you always trust. But Beatriz is Latin, and Bob, Roberto, is *muy alegre* (very lively). Only now Roberto will be so tired from the big scandal that he will not have energies to flirt, even should he have the chance. And Beatriz will know that he is *muy serio* (very dignified) now, for a long time. By the time this wears off . . ."

"What will you do next time, Mamacita?"

"I don't know yet . . . but I will think of something!"

And nearly fifty years of successful marriage sparkled in her big black eyes, as she smiled and dimpled at me.

Thus I learned that jealousy is a useful and revered emotion in Mexico, and made to earn its way.

One time when I was at the house of my friend Margarita, her brother, who had been in the United States studying engineering, came in and sat down, and began to chat very amiably.

"The American women are wonderful," he said, undertaking to flatter me and to impress Margarita at the same time. "They are daughters, but they are also companions to their father. They are sisters, and at the same time companions to their brothers. They are sweethearts, and at the same time companions to their man!"

"Well," commented Margarita tartly, "thank God we still have two sexes in Mexico!"

"But Margarita," he protested, "the men like this companionship! The wife goes with them hunting; she helps make the camp; she accompanies them on the fishing trips; she makes the business journeys. They are always together!"

But Margarita was not impressed.

"Poor American men," she sighed, "if they can never get away from the women! They must get terribly bored."

"Oh no! They . . ."

"But they divorce very much. Could it not be that they tire of this companion who is with them like their right hand all day and all night?"

"No, you do not understand. This friendliness is part of American life. Friendliness between men and women."

"If I were to meet a man who wanted me to be friends with him, I would never speak to him again in my life!" exploded Margarita, in outraged womanhood. "For either he is lying and intends to trick me later, or he is not a man! Friends indeed! For a friend I want somebody to help me with my embroidery, to choose with me a color for my nail polish, a person with whom I can read sad poetry and cry. Would a man friend do this?"

"Of course not! You . . ."

"But if I am expected to help load the gun and clean the fish and change the tire, I am entitled to some reciprocity, am I not?"

"Well, you see . . ."

"It is just as in Mexico. Everything for the man, and no reciprocity. Only here it is more natural, for the man never pretends to be anything he is not. Nor the woman either."

The brother was now getting angry.

"You refuse to understand," he shouted. "There the people believe in equality between the sexes!"

"What an absurd idea," scoffed Margarita. "When everybody knows the woman is worth ten of every man, in everything except fighting and playing poker. And what woman wants to go to war or play poker?"

"It is written on the law books that women may have the same rights as men," continued the brother, warming to his theme. "They may vote, and they may have the control of their children."

"Oh, men are so impractical," answered Margarita impatiently. "They never see farther than their noses. So women may vote? And for whom? For the people the men choose as candidates, is it not so? And what good does it have that women's rights are written down in the law books? Any woman worth her salt can make her men love her so dearly that they will do far more for her than the law says they must. And it is far much more agreeable."

So much for the provincial Mexican woman's attitude toward law and all the elaborate ritual of legality that delights men. For this reason, independence in the female, a quality much appreciated in the United States, is not considered admirable to the same extent in Mexico. The idea is that when women are foolish enough to make themselves independent, nobody will look after them any more, and that it is nicer to be looked after.

No matter how brave she is (and I have seen a Mexican girl snatch off her shoe and go after a rattler with it), the *provinciana* will melt down into feminine frailty the minute a pair of pants appears on the horizon. It is considered sound common sense, nothing more.

Mamacita explained this to me.

"People have to practice, Eleesabet," she told me. "Men are not very brave, otherwise God would have arranged that they bear the children. But you see what God did, and God cannot err. Name me one man anywhere who would have borne ten children, without one drop of anaesthetic. So it is up to the women to make them practice being valiant, otherwise they would all drink themselves to death or have heart attacks whenever there was trouble. So let them, every day or every week, do something that strengthens their will against pain or danger; it is very good for them. And also," she added sagely, "the man who performs a brave act before a lady will love her very much, for she has seen him do it. But if instead, she pushes him away and acts with courage to save him from some physical danger, he will feel robbed of his virility, and he will never feel toward her in the same way.

"Do not look so proud, *hijita*. I am telling you what has

been known in Mexico for six centuries, and in Spain for twenty."

But I was not convinced all along the line.

Part of the Mexican woman's program of pampering the men, to keep them brave and happy, is the fiction that no wife can bear to eat a mouthful of food if her husband isn't present. If this started out as a stratagem to make consciences lash the husbands home on time for lunch and dinner, it doesn't work that way. They stroll in when they please. And it is expected that everything shall be served to them hot and delicious, on the instant, and that the lady of the house will eat by her lord's side.

I still had a considerable store of American independence left in me, despite many wise counsels, and one day when my husband didn't appear for lunch by two o'clock, I assumed he had made other plans, and I sat down and ate mine.

The servant was annoyed with me, and my husband was startled speechless. However, he soon learned that the little woman ate at her regular hours, and he seemed able to get home for lunch and dinner quite punctually thereafter. My cook thought me a monster, and when I confessed to my Mexican friends that I got hungry at the usual time, whether my lord and master was present or not, they all looked at me in great pity and distrust.

But so ingrained is this habit, that Mexican food is all of the type that can be kept hot for hours without spoiling taste or texture, and dinner may be served at eight, nine, ten, eleven or midnight, whenever *el señor* deigns to arrive.

Companionship between men and women is looked at

askance in Mexico. So is the great American plan of being "a pal" to your children.

Mexicans believe, I found, that you can have affection or respect, or both, but if forced to choose, they would plump for respect. In Mexican homes it is definitely Mamacita and Papacito who rule the roost. Children are cuddled and pampered and adored—but they are made to obey.

How this is achieved I do not know, for I have rarely seen a Mexican parent administer a physical punishment (except a pinch) to a child. But scolding is a terrible weapon. There have been cases when a child committed suicide after a scolding. Servants will disappear from a house where they are working, if they think they may get a scolding for some peccadillo. To be scolded causes tears to rise, even to the eyes of men over thirty. It is just unbearable, it is simply fierce!

The somewhat pitiful—to my mind almost tragic— spectacle of parents in fear of their offspring, is not seen in Mexico.

I have observed Americans in Mexico jittering about in mortal terror of their children's opinions, hovering on their judgments, not daring to plan anything for their own pleasure, but being grateful if the youths of the family give them any of their valuable time. They wag their tails when the kids throw them a bone.

Here it is the other way around. The young people are much preoccupied to secure the good opinion of Mamacita and Papacito.

Thinking this all over very carefully, I decided to go Mexican in a number of ways.

I don't lay out Luis's clothes for him, choose his tie, and help dress him (as many good Mexican wives do), but then my friend Carmen advised me not to do this, telling me that it was not worth the extra affection one gained by it. I eat my lunch when I'm hungry, but I pretend that I can't sup without him by my side. We have always had a cook, but he insists that not one can cook an egg, and I therefore take the skillet and fry his egg with my transcendental skill, and serve it to him myself, shoring up much credit. I am a veteran mouse killer, ferocious and bloodthirsty, but when I hear a squeak now, I jump up on a chair and let my big brave husband go for the cat. I have learned to administer a scolding that sends chills up and down my own back.

But my husband, on the strength of the breakfast egg, thinks the house would fall down if I weren't in it to preside over the table; and until the end of my days I expect to hear only an affectionate "Yes, Mamacita!" whenever I hold up my ear trumpet and demand an answer to my speeches.

When I am aged and tiresome, and ring my bell for attention all day, and throw down my water glass in a temper and refuse to eat my soup, my Mexican sons will consult in soft voices. But they will be saying "*Pobrecita de Mamacita,* she is nervous today. You go to town to buy her some brandied cherries and I'll run across the street and borrow a whodunit to read to her," instead of "Do you think, if we gave up whisky, we could afford to rent her a room in the Shady Rest Home for Troublesome Old Ladies?"

Yes, in many ways, I have become thoroughly Mexican.

XIX

ONE DAY WHEN Luis and I were visiting a town in central Mexico we saw a parade of cotton-clad Indians go by. They were walking roughly in formation, their sandaled or bare feet making no noise; they shuffled along in almost morose silence. No murmuring or talking in the ranks, no sudden shouts of defiance, no exuberant songs.

"Why are they marching?" I asked.

"They don't know," answered my husband.

"What do you mean? They must have some idea!" I protested.

"Well, we'll find out," replied Luis, and he stepped up to one of the Indians and detained him gently.

"Excuse me, comrade," he said politely, "but why are you marching? What is the reason for the parade?"

The Indian snatched off his straw hat in courtesy.

"Who knows, patron?" he answered. "They told us to march."

"Who told you?"

The Indian waved his hand vaguely toward the rear.

"Some *señores*, back there."

Then he resumed his place and docilely continued the procession.

I thought I had learned something, but Luis solemnly warned me, and gave me an exposition of the Mexican view about the Indians who are left. Most of them have been absorbed into the race and the civilization; only about ten percent remain pure, and dedicated to the life they have always known.

As a Mexican Luis sees the Indians without the sentimentality that afflicts most foreigners in their first contacts with them, and without race prejudice, since Indian blood runs in nearly all Mexican veins. They are simply a group of his countrymen. The fact that Luis is a salesman tinges his understanding of the traditional Indian "stubbornness."

"The Indians seem very docile, gentle, and obedient," Luis told me, "but this just shows how clever they are. It saves them trouble. They are much smarter than the people who have tried to exploit them. They have defended their own ways through generations, by seeming to conform, by apparently yielding. The Conquerors came, the Viceroys, the missionary priests, the Independence, the Reform . . . and a certain number of the Indians live as they always have and always will."

"But how did they manage to hold out against all those forces for change?" I wanted to know.

"Sales resistance," said Luis. "They are masters of it. They simply don't want the things we think they should want, and they won't work to get them. Whenever any individual among them wants something, he gets it, for they are brilliant, and many of our greatest minds have been pure Indian. But they like their own ways, and they won't work long hours or dress differently or eat differently, or conform in any way except to certain things like vaccination, which they see is useful. They don't want ice boxes and cars and washing machines. Once in a while they want a radio. Because they like music. But they move it into their hut, and never worry about other things to go with it. They think we are all mad to work ourselves to death for so many useless things."

"And yet they are so very devout," I murmured. "They did accept the religion brought by the Spaniards."

"Yes, but it strengthened their deepest feelings, their instinctive distrust of material wealth. The priest they loved best they called 'Motolinia' which means 'Poor Man.' The religion of Jesus is one of self-denial, and of turning away from earthly comforts. Our Indians, a spiritual race, accepted this. And they noticed that when Our Lady appeared, it was not to some fat and rich *hacendado,* but to Juan Diego, one of their own, humble and poor as themselves. The Indians confound everybody with their literal Christianity. They drive the social uplifters crazy when they want to make them more healthy, improve their conditions of life, and get them into new clean housing units. They say, of everything that happens to them, even when they lose a baby because of some preventable disease, 'It is God's will.'

"It is sales resistance, and this literal Christianity, that preserves them from change and from absorption. Whenever you ask one to do anything for you, he says he will 'if God permits,' and if you tell him to come early to work in the morning he answers, 'I will, if God wants me to.' *Si Dios quiere.*"

I had a lesson in Indian sales resistance from one of my maids, not long after. Her name was Blanca, and she was a quick and clever girl who could do anything well. She cooked so nicely that I said to her one day, "Hortensia wants to go back to live on the rancho. If you will cook and also do the cleaning, I will pay you both salaries."

"No, *señora, muchas gracias.*"

"It won't be too much work. I will help you."

"No, *señora,* I prefer to work less, even if I earn less."

Nothing could shake her in her calm decision. She didn't want more clothes, she had enough. Shoes? She had a pair that didn't hurt at all. Movies? She would rather go for a walk on the other side of the river with her sweetheart. Cosmetics? Her sweetheart wouldn't allow her to wear them anyhow. A permanent wave? She had had one once but she didn't like it, and now she wore her braids as before. To save for her old age? She was going to marry her Juan and God would look after them when they were old, or their children would.

Sales resistance.

Some weeks later Luis and I observed the same kind of parade, and it seemed to us, with the identical Indians, in Monterrey.

"But this is odd," said Luis aloud, puzzled. "Because we have no Indians like this here in the north. Our people are all *mestizo,* and mostly they are factory workers or ranch hands, and they dress in *mezclilla* (blue jeans) and wear shoes. I wonder who brought these poor fellows to march here in Monterrey?"

We were not long in finding out. It was a Communist demonstration, we learned from the papers in the evening. Five thousand "workers" had demonstrated against the Monterrey industrialists before the governor's house. They had been harangued by *liders* and the thrifty hard-working *Regiomontanos* had been called a hundred bad names.

In order to explain the Communist demonstration which had been performed by hundreds of docile Indians from a neighboring state who had been gathered up and hauled to the scene by professional organizers, I will have to explain something of the peculiar history of Monterrey.

Monterrey today is a prosperous industrial city, full of busy factories and burgeoning industry. It grew to its present position as Queen Industrial City of Mexico through the sheer hard work and energy of all the *Regio-montanos,* the industrialists who were ready to develop new industries at risk to themselves, and the workmen who were willing to labor and to share in the prosperity, as it came. It alone among the great cities of Mexico, was not a port, nor set amidst lush agricultural lands or woods, or near rich mines. The land is semi arid, there are no mines, and the soil itself offers no basic wealth to be developed. Why then was it settled and how did it come to its present eminence?

For the explanation of this we have to look far back into the turbulent history of Spain.

Queen Isabel, who had given Columbus the support he needed to set sail and discover the New World, and her husband, King Ferdinand, were beginning the unification of Spain under Catholicism. The long wars against the Moors were expensive, and the organization of the United Catholic Kingdoms, and the consolidation of the colonial wealth, were costly. Ferdinand and Isabel, the Catholic monarchs, found their coffers empty. But there were many wealthy Jews in Spain. The "expulsion" was not merely an act of religious fanaticism. It made it legal for the crown to forfeit any properties of Jews who refused conversion.

To cover the crassness of this "expropriation," Isabel

had been made to think that the expulsion was a religious necessity, to preserve unity and save Spain from division under many faiths. Therefore it followed that if the Jews consented to be baptized they need not lose the protection of the Crown. Thus many thousands of Jews took the Catholic faith and became what were called "The New Christians." Some really were converts and pious devotees; others merely conformed in order to save their properties, and continued to practice the faith of their fathers in secret synagogues. Upon these, who pretended to be Christians in order to share in the protection of the state, while secretly "Judaizing," the wrath of the Inquisition fell, in all its terror.

In 1579 a brave captain, Luis de Carbajal y de la Cueva, a fervent Catholic, son of New Christians, was given permission by the crown to go and conquer some lands which lay to the north in Mexico. He subdued the Indians in the region, and baptized them, and founded the city which became the "Metropolitan City of Our Lady of the Immaculate Conception of Monterrey."

Carbajal was not happy in his marriage, for his wife, Doña Guiomar, was an ardent Jewess, who never ceased to beg her husband to return to the ways of his ancestors. She would not accompany him to the New World, but begged him to take many of her friends and relatives who, she said, wanted to seek their fortune in the New World. She swore to Don Luis that all were Christians.

But secretly she exhorted a niece, Isabel, who accompanied them, to be sure to hold them all firmly to their Jewish faith and all its rituals. In the lists of the men who accompanied Don Luis on his conquests, and who settled in or near Monterrey, the names are all "New Christian"

names, the names of Jews who wanted a fresh start in the
world, some of them to face the world as Catholic Christians, others to return, they thought in safety, to their own
religion.

The names of those men are the same names that
dominate trade, industry, and government in Monterrey
today. Names like Sada, Montemayor, Garza, de la Garza,
Treviño, Gonzalez, Martinez . . .

Thus it is not fantasy but fact when the Monterrey
people are referred to as "the Jews of Mexico," though all
are Catholics today.

Yet long before modern industrial Monterrey had begun to rise out of sound Jewish knowledge of markets,
banking, trade, and credits, many a novel—romantic, bloody,
cruel, and strange—had been lived out by the New Christians and their sons and daughters.

The Holy Inquisition moved to Mexico and it pursued
with ferocity any "relapsed Judaizers." Don Luis de Carbajal, then governor of what is now Nuevo Leon, was
accused by his own relatives, taken to Mexico and impris-
oned and tortured, to make him confess. He died in
prison, a steadfast Catholic to the end.

But his nephews and nieces, who had been secret and
ardent Jews, died on the *porto* (a kind of rack), or in
prison, taking with them, through the confessions exacted
under torture, dozens of companions. "Luis Carbajal el
mozo," a nephew of the ill-fated governor, lived out a life
of haunted fear and misery before he died confessing his
sins as a relapsed Jew. And there was brave old Tomas
Treviño, who was burned at the stake, after the Inquisition
had taken from him his immense wealth and had dis-
graced him publicly for worshiping in a secret synagogue.

"Throw on more wood," he shouted in defiance, at his tormentors. "I've paid for it, a thousand ducats an inch!" And he would not recant.

This then is the type of man who founded Monterrey. Jews in their blood and bones, though they all became Catholics with the passing of the years. The families intermarried closely, and Monterrey is still something of an ethnic island in Spanish-Indian-*mestizo* Mexico.

Hard workers, traders and organizers, thrifty and persevering, the *Regiomontanos* had also their racial passion for social betterment, and they put various forms of it into operation as the city began its industrial rise. They led the republic in housing plans for workmen, in cooperatives to save workmen money on purchase of clothes and foodstuffs, in opening to workmen the right to purchase preferred stock in the industry, after a fixed number of years as an employee. They built schools and theaters and sports fields for their workmen. They paid consistently higher wages than anywhere else in the republic.

The Monterrey Jews then were in no mood to have organizers from outside arrive in Monterrey by train, harangue the workmen to join the Communist Party and share the wealth, and then take the next train back. It put their backs up.

And after a "Communist demonstration" was performed, with the tacit blessing of Mexico City, by groups of gentle Indians from other states, who had just gone along for the ride and the free lunch, the *Regiomontanos* got fighting mad.

They demanded the right to stage their own "anti-Communist" demonstration. Mexico City, however, at that time rather tender toward Reds in general, withheld the permission.

So the word went round by underground that Monterrey was going to show how it felt about Communists, permission or no. There would be an anti-Communist parade, anyhow.

I got the word from Mamacita who found the drama and the defiance of it, the secret preparations for it, grist to her plot-loving soul.

"Eleesabet," she whispered, over the phone, "can you hear me?"

"Almost, Mamacita."

"Tomorrow we must march!"

"Yes, Mamacita? Where?"

"To the Palace of the Governor! You will come to my house at ten o'clock tomorrow morning!"

"I'll be there."

When I arrived at Bolivar 492 next morning at 10, Mamacita met me at the door. She was pale with importance and rage. She was wearing her second-best black silk dress, and had her hair dressed high and held with a small tortoiseshell comb. She drew me in, hissing, "We are going to defy Mexico City!"

I started in some perturbation, for I had heard Mamacita recommend that various civil disorders would be quickly fixed up if they would just shoot two or three, and see how fast the rest behaved themselves. She had seen the revolution and rather liked parts of it.

"Yesterday the Communists marched, a few hundred miserable Inditos, who do as they are told," she said. "Today, we march!"

"We?" I quavered.

"We free *Regiomontanos!* The members of the Acción

Cívica (Civic Action)!" This was an orderly local group which took some part in politics.

Various ladies of Mamacita's age, rather fluttery and frightened until they were fired by Mamacita's excitement, arrived. Mamacita took her place in front and we all went out into the street. It was already filling with men, women, children, servants. People were pouring out of their houses to join the parade. Mamacita's eyes snapped with martial fervor. Her dimples kept popping in and out. She stood very straight and marched with great military precision on her French-heeled size-2 slippers.

Soon Bolivar Street was packed solid. We surged into Hidalgo, adding numbers all the while, and were about to pour into Zaragoza Plaza.

"Mamacita! Your blood pressure!" It was Luis, who had come pelting after us, and had finally pushed his way through the crowd and to our side. He made us let the procession go on without us, but this gave us a buffeting that would have been worse than going with the stream. He gave up and we tumbled into Zaragoza Plaza with all the rest. It was evident that the city had turned out en masse. It was impossible to get near the Palace of the Governor; streets converging on the square were one heaving, milling, defiant throng. Then orders came through from Mexico City to arrest "the persons demonstrating without a license."

No police could have thrown the entire city in jail; no jail would hold all the demonstrators. But the crowd gave a shout of joy at the news and all able-bodied men cheerfully marched off to the Military City (an enormous barracks) and placed themselves under arrest.

Monterrey was at that time a city of about 100,000 inhabitants. From rich land owners and factory managers down through the doctors and lawyers, students, and the workers from the factories (thousands of them), everybody was in jail. Wives stayed home at the request of their husbands, but presented themselves for roll-taking. The city of Monterrey was in jail, and glad of it. The Acción Cívica was rampant.

There was high wassail. Orchestras were formed. There were dances. Restaurant crews got together and prepared succulent banquets. Leading citizens addressed their fellow prisoners in passionate orations. The dismayed soldiers posted to guard the illegal anti-Communist demonstrators were unnerved by the festivities. There was a sharp exchange of notes between the authorities and Mexico City, the capital of the Federal government.

"All are arrested. What shall I do with them?" was the anguished cry from enforcement officers in Monterrey.

Mexico City decided to let the malcreants off with fines. But the prisoners to a man refused to pay fines, and demanded trials.

At last the whole thing got so out of hand that Mexico City gave up, ordered "Let them all go" and was glad to get the stiff-necked *Regiomontanos* back into their homes and about their business before foreign newsreel companies got wind of the situation and descended to take pictures that would confer on the Federal government, the ultimate horror . . . the danger of appearing ridiculous.

Mamacita and all the other fiery anti-Communist ladies prepared parties of rejoicing and general celebrations to welcome home their proud jailbirds. Our group consisted of thirty people. Papacito as usual had his chair at the head of the table, with his dog Diana sitting on the floor at his left and Galatea his cat, on his right. The table was decorated with flowers and streamers of colored paper. There were four kinds of tamales, chocolate, *buñuelos* (a delicious fried cake), cake made with eighteen eggs, the *cocada* (a coconut sweet) made from the recipe of Doña Dolores, Mamacita's great grandmother, and *marquesotas* made by Tia Rosa. You couldn't hear yourself think with all the shouting back and forth, the laughing and the excitement. Similar scenes were being enacted in every home in Monterrey.

Luis whispered to me, "They are remembering when the Federal government did something else they didn't like, and the whole city joined together and had a taxpayers' strike!"

"But how could they?"

"They could because they all stand together. The whole town held firm. You have seen that it is impossible to discipline an entire city. The government had to give in.

"Another time all the citizens just declared that they would not buy anything except the barest necessities of food, until the government ceded in an important matter. This was when the churches were closed by Federal order. So nobody in Monterrey went to the movies, or bought dresses or underclothing or shoes or furniture, or anything whatsoever except a little beans and meat. What happened? The merchants lost money and could not pay their taxes, and because Monterrey is a rich city, the Federal government felt the lack of taxes at once. And they quietly allowed us to open enough churches in which to worship."

"It's wonderful, such civic courage."

"You see, the answer is this. Everybody in the republic

makes fun of us *Regiomontanos* because we love money. Okay, we do. But so do they! And how they squeal whenever anybody is astute enough to injure them in the pocketbook!

"Think it over. Just what would happen if the city of, let us say, Detroit, withheld taxes!"

"I guess there would be a civil war."

"That I doubt," said Luis. "But some sort of immediate 'compromise' would be worked out, you can bet."

Papacito put in a word. He was taking only tea made of *manzanilla* blossoms, for he had so much indigestion, so much oppression in the chest, lately.

"Eleesabet understands about civic courage," he said. "About the anger of citizens against galling restrictions imposed by a far-away government. Didn't you work in the town where they held that famous Tea Party, *hijita?*"

He stopped to feed a tidbit to Galatea, who was expecting again.

"Women are more of a power in these fights than they seem, too," he mused. "Take Mamacita, for instance. Actually, she doesn't care too much about the principle of the thing. But she's a brave and adventurous woman, and she doesn't have much chance to indulge this side of her character, here in her quiet patio, among her ferns and flowers.

"But she has enormous courage, all the same. If you don't believe me, try walking down the length of Bolivar Street on a hot day in shoes a size too small for you!"

XX

I HAVE A DEAR friend named Rose who lives in Boston, who has never forgotten my birthday, no matter where in the wide world I have been wandering. Always some package arrives with her loving remembrance.

On my birthday in Monterrey, I received a notice that a package was waiting for me in the postoffice. I thought of course it must be from Rose. So I happily put on my hat and walked over to the Independencia Square, where the postoffice sits on a slight incline, looking down over the city.

I marched up to a window and presented my notice that a package had been sent me.

"Your identification?" asked the clerk.

I hadn't brought any identification, so I turned around and walked home again.

At lunchtime I showed the notice to Luis who studied it carefully. "Wait for me," he said. "We will go together to find out about this package."

But next day he had forgotten my package, and I having nothing to do, so I thought to myself, I will take my driving license as identification, and go and ask for my package by myself.

I went up to the same window and showed my driving license.

"This is a foreign document," said the clerk sternly. "I cannot admit it as evidence."

I slunk away.

At lunchtime I confessed to Luis that I had again gone to the postoffice and what had happened there.

"You haven't got any identification, I suppose," he said thoughtfully. "That is, no Mexican identification. I will have to go and take you with me, and swear before a notary that you are my wife."

"But good heavens," I protested wildly. "All this row over what is probably a little hand-made cotton apron!"

"We are dealing with the most ruthless and complicated system in the whole complicated Mexican Government," said Luis. "People have gone to get packages from the post office, carrying their identification and when their starved corpse is found, years later, the document helps their families to identify them, so they can take them away to be buried. Why . . ."

"It can't possibly be as bad as that!"

"I've heard that it is a little worse in Central China," admitted Luis.

So we went back with Luis's identification, and a copy of our marriage lines.

"This was a foreign marriage," commented the clerk. "Not legal in Mexico. You must show a certificate of Mexican civil marriage."

This was before Luis and I had got married again in front of the Civil Registrar; we had no idea at the time, that this was so crucial.

"We will go and get you a Mexican driving license," said resourceful Luis. "That ought to do it."

So I went to the Palace of Government, made an

appointment for my medical examination next day and an appointment with the examiner who was to find out that I really knew how to drive. In about a week's time, I had the license, with my picture and thumb print on it, the proper stamps, certificate of payment of fee, etc., etc., etc. With this firmly clutched I went back and faced the postoffice clerk again.

He ruefully admitted that I was to all intents and purposes to be identified as Elizabeth Borton de Treviño and that I apparently had the right to receive the package addressed to a person of that name. Or at least to take the next step. It seemed they didn't just hand over the package. Too simple.

I was given a bit of paper with a number on it and sent to another window. When my turn came, the clerk looked at me severely and asked, "Who sent you this package?"

"Why it says on the notice that the point of origin is Boston, so I thought perhaps my friend Rose . . ." I babbled.

He drew out his papers and consulted them.

"No," he said, looking at me over the tops of his glasses. "Not Rose."

"Well, I have no idea. I have lots of friends. Various people send me presents . . ."

"What is in this package?"

"How do I know?" I shouted. "It was sent to me, wasn't it? But I haven't been allowed to get near it! How should I know what's in it?"

I glared, and he looked pained. I had yet to learn that when you lose your temper in dealing with the bureaucracy in Mexico you merely set yourself back. He calmly beckoned to the person behind me in line, and there was nothing for me to do but go home and take a little *boldo* tea to calm my liver (that was boiling like an angry sea) and wait for Luis.

Again we took up the matter of my war with the post-office and worked out a fresh strategy.

Luis said, "It is now a little difficult. Of course you could just let the notice lapse and then the package would either be confiscated or go back to the person who sent it. If it goes back to the person who sent it, you will probably get a letter asking what to do with it."

"I'm not going to give up yet," I gritted through my teeth.

"Well, when you go back to the postoffice, be a little bit more feminine about the whole thing. Say you can't imagine what the package can be. Act helpless and they may give you a tiny hint. Cry a little bit."

I went back to the postoffice, wearing a ruffled blouse, and a picture hat. I took my place in the line. I presented my notice.

"Your identification?"

I presented it.

"What is in this package?"

"A surprise to me! You see, we were just married, that is, not so long ago, and it must be a gift!" I leaned over close and shone my eyes on the granite-faced gentleman in the window. "I hope it is a box of wedding silver!"

He thawed a little, and said sadly, "I'm afraid it is not silver."

"Oh, what a disappointment!" I allowed my chin to quiver. He became agitated and said, "Now, now!"

I braced up a little, and seemed to get a grip on myself.

"Do you smoke?" he asked me.

"Why, why, sometimes! That is, I used to! My husband doesn't like me to, in Mexico."

"Different customs."

"That's right. My husband is Mexican and I try to adopt his ways."

"Please your husband. That's a good rule." Here he leaned over confidentially and whispered, as the line grew longer and people shuffled their feet behind me. "Well, *señora,* this package contains *a carton of American cigarettes!*"

"Oh, lovely!" I clapped my hands. "Luis will be so glad!"

"But there is—a difficulty."

"Another difficulty?"

"You are not allowed to import cigarettes."

"Import? But I haven't imported anything. I had no idea anybody was sending me cigarettes."

"Well, I am going to let you make out this special solicitude, this special request, to the postmaster, asking that you be allowed to receive the package. It's irregular. But I will make an exception in your case." And he handed me a sheaf of papers, four or five sheets of carbon paper, and a stubby pencil.

"Go over there and sit down and make out the forms," he directed me. "Take your time and answer all the questions carefully. This will have to go to the head of the Customs Department. That is, if the postmaster approves it."

I took my papers and sat down. It took me about an hour to read it through, for it was all fine print, and I had been brought up by a lawyer father to read all the fine print. Then I adjusted all the carbons and painstakingly

answered all the questions, writing down my age, where I
was born, name of father and mother, their professions,
their religion, their nationality, my husband's profession,
his religion, his nationality. And so on. Rather cross eyed
from my toil among the fine print I went back, got in line
again, and smilingly handed the man in the window my
papers.

He handed them right back to me.

"Go upstairs, down the hall and turn to the right. You
will come to an ante-room. There you may ask for an
appointment with the postmaster. When you see him, you
must give him your solicitude."

I followed directions carefully. In the waiting room
were several other shell-shocked citizens who had received
some kind of package from abroad and whose lives would
never be the same again.

A secretary sat there taking down names and addresses
and dispensing little appointment cards with numbers on
them. My number was 23. After a while a door opened
and a woman in widow's weeds emerged from the inner
office. The next number was called. It was 14. My heart
sank. But I settled down to wait. If I did not turn up at
home, Luis at least knew where to send the search parties.

When at last my number was called, I arose to my now
numb feet and staggered in.

A calm gray-haired gentleman received my papers, read
them through, and shook his head gravely over some
points.

Then he said, "You will receive an official acknow-
ledgment of these documents in a few days." He got up
and bowed, and I was released into the world again.

When I recounted to Luis everything that had happened, he said, "Now my advice is to relax and forget the whole matter. If some day you receive an official paper of some kind, we will then see what is to be done."

I followed my husband's counsel and life went on as before. I knitted leggings for the Little General, so that he could play on the cool tiles without catching cold. Poli brought me presents of dry leaves and dead cockroaches. I daily wrote to my parents, urging them to come and visit me. And I again tried to learn to make *tortillas*, patting the dough between my palms, but again I was a total failure.

About three weeks later I got an official envelope. I laid this on the lunch table at Luis's place and asked him as my attorney, to open and read it.

He read the letter inside and told me that it said that my solicitude to receive a certain package had been received and would be acted upon in good time.

"I will lock this up in my strong box," said Luis, "for they admit that they have your package and that they received your solicitude to receive your package. Now we've got something on them. We've almost got a case."

"But don't I *do* anything?" I wailed.

"Not a thing but sit tight. Before we get through, we may be asked to leave the country as undesirables. We must act cautiously and be very careful what we say from now on."

Finally one day I got another notice from the post-office, this time ordering me to appear before the postmaster.

I went, showed my identification, got in several lines, was handed an appointment card, and finally was received. The postmaster handed me back my original solicitude, now decorated with many seals and countersigns, and informed me that I would now be allowed to pay the duties, affix the stamps, and see my package.

I was told to present myself at window 10 with a carbon copy of my solicitude, which he then pressed into my eager hand. He kept the originals with the ribbons and seals.

At window 10 I again filled out a special form, under the coaching of the clerk and then I was told to go to window 21, get in line, and buy a certain number of stamps, of a specified value. By this time I was beginning to understand why Mexico has no unemployment.

This operation of buying the stamps took some time. After I had them, I was placed in charge of a gentleman who wore an enormous key suspended on a cord from his belt. He led me up to a strange sort of cell, a kind of cage of stout wire, with a tiny opening in it at eye height. Into this cage I was locked with my stamps, and the man with the key went away.

"This is what I get for mixing myself up with the post-office department," I muttered to myself, and I wondered whether I would be exposed to public censure inside my cage or put on a train and deported in it.

But behold, the man with the keys returned, and through the small window he pushed some documents and a pen. These papers said that I swore a mighty oath that I had received my package and that it was in good order.

I should not have signed this, for I had not received my package, but I was in a cage, and I was too weak to fight any more. I signed.

Then through the little window, at last, came my battered package.

"Open it," I was ordered.

With trembling fingers I undid the strings and knots. Inside was a carton of Chesterfields, and a card which said, "Love from Marian." I had to show the card to the guard, but he decided, after due thought, to let me keep it. He then told me how to stick each stamp on each package of cigarettes in such a way that when the package was opened, the stamps would be torn. I did this all very carefully, conscious of the guard's suspicious eye on me. He then took all the cigarettes away from me, turned a key in the lock, and let me out. "Window 17," he said.

I went to window 17. I again showed my notice, my identification, my solicitude, and copy of the paper which said I had received my package in good order. The man with the key whispered in the ear of the man in window 17, and I was given more papers to sign and told to pay one peso and seventeen cents storage charges.

Then they gave me my package.

I stumbled home and threw myself on my bed, and called for an ice cap. While I lay there promising to be a good girl for years and years if I would only be spared any more trials like this one, the doorbell rang and Blanca went to answer it. She came back with a little pink card. A notice from the post office that a package was waiting for me, origin Los Angeles.

I tore the little card into very small pieces.

XXI

W HAT WE HAD hoped for was about to come to pass. My father and mother planned to visit us. The whole Treviño tribe was alerted. Special seeds were planted at Papacito's ranch, the Banco de las Flores, so that they should be blooming when Mrs. Borton arrived. The road to the *ranchito* from the main highway was worked over, and rocks and roots carted away, so that there should be no injury to Mr. Borton's car, driving up there. Parties were planned, and Jorge, Luis's brother in Mexico City who was an actor and singer in the movies, was sent for, to make sure that entertainment should not flag.

I turned my house upside down to clean it. In the midst of this, Hortensia my cook came and said she had to be away for two days, on very urgent business.

When Luis arrived home that evening I placed before him an American supper. Recognizing my biscuits he asked, "Where is Hortensia?"

"She had to go away for a couple of days, to her village."

Luis slapped his brow with the flat of his hand.

"Now what will you do? With your mother and father arriving on Thursday?"

"Hortensia promised to be back day after tomorrow."

"You will never hear from her again," he told me flatly. But Luis for once was wrong about his people and I was right. Hortensia appeared, broadly smiling, when she had promised, her arms loaded with queer stone implements, buckets and packages. Right behind her was a small brown boy bearing a large and lifelike pig's head, and behind him, another smaller boy, with several sacks of what turned out to be dried corn shucks. The procession passed the astounded Luis who at once demanded what was up.

"*Tamales*," said Hortensia. "I will make *tamales* for the Señora Grande."

Señora Grande meant the big or the older *señora*, in short, my mother. I had been demoted to Señora Chica, or little *señora*.

"She'll be slaving over those until midnight and most of tomorrow," said Luis, who knew the procedure. "We'll eat out or with Mamacita, and not bother her."

I did the housework while Hortensia was busy in the kitchen, for Blanca was pressed into service to help her and the two small brothers were in and out all day on various errands.

First Hortensia washed and scraped and barbered the hog's head and at last put it on to boil with various savory spices, many of which I had never seen before. Meanwhile the corn which she had brought in buckets, had to be put to soak in lime, and then washed in several waters and then ground by hand, handful by handful on the ancient stone *metate* (or grinding stone), a prehistoric vessel, for the like has been found in caves under the lava flow near Mexico City, which came from an eruption of Mount Ajusco ten centuries before Christ. The washed corn may be ground by machinery, in a *molino* or mill for the purpose, but these tamales were to be very special and fine ones, and everything had to be done by hand in the traditional way.

To do the grinding Hortensia knelt on the floor over her *metate*, and rolled the grains with a stone *metlapil*, or rolling pin, all the weight of her body coming down on each stroke of the stone against stone. When she was weary the little boys would spell her. I offered to help too but I was waved away. I wouldn't know how, they said.

After the corn was all ground Hortensia put it into a great clean washtub and began to beat into it softened pure lard, salt and the gelatinous broth from the hog's head. This beating had to be done in a special way for the broth and the lard were to flavor and enrich the corn while the beating was to lighten it, on the same principle as beaten biscuits. I was shoved aside from this beating, too. It became clear that the *tamales* were to be a labor of love and respect for the Señora Grande, Hortensia's contribution to this wonderful visit.

Leaving a small boy beating the corn, Hortensia got busy with the *chiles*. These were first toasted in a flame until they gave off a delicious scent, spicy and appetizing; then they were opened and seeded and wrapped in wet towels. After some time in the damp cloths, the *chiles* were taken out. Now the tough toasted outer skin could be peeled away with the fingers, leaving the fleshy pulp of the pepper. Hortensia reluctantly allowed me to make myself useful at this, while she set to work on the hog's head. Every particle of meat and fat and gelatine was now cut carefully into very small pieces with a sharp knife. (Some lazy people grind the meat and fat but to Hortensia this was anathema; each particle should have its own flavor and not be all mauled up and pre-digested.) Then this delicate and flavorsome meat was set aside temporarily. Not in an icebox, for that would ruin it, congeal the fat, and change its texture. It was set in a cool window and the dish was covered with a clean cloth.

Next the *chiles,* peeled, were put on the *metate,* sprinkled with rock salt, cummin seeds and various dry leaves of savory plants, and ground down to a soft uniform paste.

Into a great *cazuela* (a cooking vessel made of baked clay), Hortensia put lard, and when it was hissing, in went the paste of *chiles* and spices. Here it had to cook and "take flavor." I was allowed to hover over this and stir and stir, while Hortensia occasionally dipped into it a bit of the broth from the hog's head. Meanwhile, she was dampening the corn husks. This too was a rite and couldn't be done just any old way.

When it was considered that the chile sauce had taken enough flavor from its slow cooking in the lard (and Hortensia had sampled it frequently, tasting daintily from a drop she dripped onto the palm of her left hand), she carefully added to it all the bits of meat previously prepared. This had to be moved in the sauce with the utmost caution, so that each tiny piece of meat should retain its shape and identity, and yet be seasoned and permeated with the rich taste of chile.

Next came the special art.

Hortensia brought in the corn shucks, moistened just right. She showed us how to proceed. She would take a leaf and holding it in the left hand, coat it to the thickness of a quarter of an inch with the prepared and beaten corn. Into this Hortensia put just the right quantity of meat in chile sauce. The leaf was then folded around the bit of meat so that the corn enclosed it, and the ends of the leaf were tucked up to form a tiny neat package, compact, but allowing room for the corn to swell. Saucers were laid upside down in the great *ollas* or jars of clay, and the little packages which were the *tamales* were then ranged round in circles, neatly packed together, until the *ollas* were full. Water was trickled under the saucers, the *ollas* were tightly covered, and fire was set under the jars until a fine steam formed. The *tamales* cooked in this steam, the corn puffing and enclosing each bite of seasoned meat.

This feast, the labor of many hours, awaited my parents next day.

I was up betimes, and had my house decked with flowers, a ribbon on Poli, and my son in clean rompers and woven sandals. It was a bright September day.

My parents phoned me from Laredo. Luis calculated that it would take them three hours to drive over, and he planned to be on the highway to guide them to my house, as neither one spoke Spanish and they would not be able to ask their way. But Mama and Papa were anxious to see their first grandson. Within two hours they drew up before my door.

"But how did you manage to find us?" I marveled, after the kisses and hugs, the first greetings and questions, the comments on how well everybody looked.

"I just said 'Treviño?' everywhere I stopped, and people would wave me forward to the next block, and suddenly, here we were," said Papa.

"Naturally," laughed Luis. "There are about a thousand Treviños in the city, and there's always bound to be one in the next block!"

Later after a cup of coffee, Papa remarked that he was pleased to see that the city of Monterrey had named so many streets after himself.

"After you?" repeated Luis, puzzled.

In the town my parents lived in, street names are written on the curbstones, but in Monterrey curbstones carry advertising. Lately they had advertised heavily a certain soap, or *jabon*, whose trade name was Supremo.

Papa, who was a famous trial lawyer and in demand as a public speaker, said, "Yes, I saw at least three streets named for me. Jawbone Supreme."

After the feast of Hortensia's tamales, we had another typical Monterrey banquet at Papacito's *ranchito*. This was the roast kid of the north of Mexico, favorite dish of all *norteños* or northerners.

The little goats are roasted on spits over open fires, and constantly dressed with a sauce of fat, garlic and sage.

While the men took care of tending the meat, the maids, under Mamacita's direction, made the favorite wheaten tortillas, and rolled them out thin, cooking them on flat plates over the coals, and cooked the *ranchero* coffee, which is made by boiling coffee and chunks of brown sugar together in a clay jar until thick. This may be drunk black, or mixed with boiling milk to make a delicious light-brown concoction. Beans, fried until they are a soft uniform *paste*, and powdered thickly with crumbs of cream cheese, finish the feast.

The *ranchito* on the hillside, the rustic house with its thatched roof, under the spreading pecan trees, the swimming pool for the children, appealed to my mother and father. Touched by Papacito's fields of daisies, my mother sent Mamacita several sacks of Holland bulbs, to be set out around the cottage at the *ranchito*. My father's letters referred often to the Banco de las Flores.

Besides the excursion to the ranchito, we took my parents down south along the highway to the sugar-cane country, to enjoy another typically Mexican festivity—a "boiling off"—at the sugar mill.

We made up several cars of friends, complete with children and dogs, and each señora brought along her measure of cinnamon, ground anise and nutmeg, vanilla, and pans of chopped pecans, as well as bars of butter, and glasses of jam.

At the roadside mills, where patient oxen or horses tramped round and round grinding the sugar cane, in a primitive platform arrangement, the freshly pressed juice is put to boil in great vats, and when it gets thick, the "puddlers" or men in charge of the vats, pour it into molds, which cast it into forms called *piloncillos*. This hard brown sugar is sold widely throughout Mexico as a sweetening, and for the making of all kinds of candies and desserts.

But the fun of a *molino* picnic was to mix the sugar with butter, spices and nuts, and then have it cast specially; one took home the conical hunks of delicious *panocha* or dark sugar candy, for treasuring against Christmas time and the festivities of the *posadas* (Christmas religious parties in the homes).

Dozens of cars would draw up around each mill, and early in the day, people would drink all they wanted of the fresh-pressed cane juice. Then the ladies would make their bargains with the tenders of the vats of boiling syrup. Some would contract to boil orange skins in the syrup and then bottle this confection; it tastes rather like a dark-complected marmalade. Others of us wanted *panocha*, and we had to be on the spot with our nuts, spices and equipment when the juice reached just the right sugaring point, or we got left, and had to wait for the next batch to be boiled. Some people liked their *piloncillos* cast mixed with guava jam; others preferred it molded around tidbits of chocolate. Every taste could be indulged. And meanwhile, there was all the fun of a Mexican *dia de campo* or picnic.

A great number of *merenderos* (rustic eating places) spring up along the highways near the sugar mills and do great business in the season of sugar molding. It was unheard of to take sandwiches to the sugar-molding parties; one always went to a *merendero* and bought plates of dark rich *enchiladas* and ice-cold beer. The children? I must report that most of them sit right up to their dish of chile and their small glass of beer like the grown folk. Though occasionally some delicate baby would be fed a dish of rice and banana.

There is an atmosphere of good fellowship and joy at these sugaring parties rather like harvest parties anywhere. One is among friends and neighbors; one is stocking his larder for the winter. The feeling is convivial and self-congratulatory.

My mother and father found all the fiestas fascinating, and they took back with them dozens of molds of dark sugar, in various flavors.

They also adored the *pulque* bread, which is a north Mexican breakfast specialty.

Pulque is the juice of the *agave* plant, or *maguey*. It

ferments quickly and is then cured with various fruit juices and flavors. Distilled into a brandy, it is the strong drink, *tequila*.

Among old-fashioned Mexican cooks, *pulque*, fermented and working, often served as a leaven, and flat loaves were made ready for the oven by mixing flour, a little lard and sugar, and plenty of the active *pulque*. The principle is more or less that of sourdough biscuits, I suppose. These long flat ovals of bread, powdered with red sugar, warm from the oven, are delicious beyond description, and my parents, having become addicted to them, wrapped up several loaves in waxed paper to take back home, also.

At the farewell party before they left for home, Papa and Mama learned a little more of Mexican provincial customs. For there was a *piñata* and a *recitadora,* lady elocutionist.

The *piñata* is a diversion for the children, which calls into play all the Mexican inventiveness and imagination. A light clay jar is filled with goodies—four-inch pieces of sugar cane, oranges, peanuts, and hard candies—and is then built into the center of some imaginative design of papier-mâché and colored tissue paper. This may be a bunny, all fluted white tissue paper, with tall pink tissue ears, or an elephant, or a fish, with trailing tissue-paper fins, or a clown, or a fairy or an angel, or anything whatsoever that the *piñata*-maker thinks of that day.

These figurines are enchantingly comic or beautiful with their gilt and silver paper streamers. By a complicated system of weights and pulleys, which all Mexicans seem to be born knowing how to arrange, the *piñata* is set up in the home, so that it hangs from the roof top, and may be lowered or drawn up at will.

Children are blindfolded, turned around three times, to make them lose their sense of direction, and then given a big decorated stick with which to try to smash the *piñata*. If there seems to be a chance that someone will really smash it before all the children have had a chance, it is pulled up out of reach. After each child has had his turn, they begin again with the littlest one, and this time, the *piñata* is not pulled out of the way. At last some child breaks it, crashes through to the jar of sweets, and breaks it, and all the contents of the jar fall out on the floor. Then ensues a terrific scramble to get some of each thing in the jar. Since all this takes place among the small fry, and brings out their destructive instincts besides, the little savages usually wind up in a fight, and there are blows and tears. But it is a part of every festivity.

After the *piñata*, we all sat in the *sala*, and a young lady who had been a pupil of a prominent elocutionist, recited poetry. My father and mother didn't understand the poetry, but the gestures, facial expressions, and vocal evolutions of the young lady fascinated them both. "It took me back fifty years to when I was made to recite 'The Boy Stood On The Burning Deck,'" confided my father. Even more amazing to my parents was the response of the young lady elocutionist's public. She evoked laughter, wags of the head, tears, applause.

The *recitadora* is very much a part of Mexican provincial life. I believe there must be as many teachers of poetry elocution, as there are piano teachers. Ladies and gentlemen, adolescents, and children, all learn to declaim, and do so with very little urging, on any occasion.

When I first went to Monterrey I thought the low thrilling tones of the voice they customarily use, the stereotyped gestures, in fact the whole idea, very corny. But as time went by, I realized that I was learning a good deal of Spanish poetry, and that it was wonderful poetry. At the time of my parents' visit I was not entirely converted. I felt something of the elocutionist's passion, but also I shared my parents' charitable amusement.

Now, of course, I am lost. I weep and applaud as madly as anybody when someone recites "La Casada Infiel" of Garcia Lorca, or "Suave Patria" of Lopez Velarde.

That last farewell party was closed *con broche de oro* (with a clasp of gold) as the Mexicans say. Jorge sang. Luis's brother Jorge is a true *tenore robusto*, one of those great ringing tenors who can't be allowed within ten feet of any microphone because he will break everybody's ear drums. Jorge had studied for opera for years in Mexico City, and he was the *pièce de résistance* that Mamacita had prepared for the delight of my parents.

After the *piñata*, after the elocutionist, Mamacita raised her brows at Jorge. He pretended not to see.

"Jorge!" she said.

"What, Mama?"

"Sing."

Jorge made the typical singer's deprecatory motions toward his throat. "A little hoarse today," he murmured.

"Sing," ordered Mamacita.

"I didn't bring my music."

"Luis can accompany you."

Despite his years of study, and his splendid voice, years of working as a comedian in the theater and in the movies have made Jorge afraid people are going to laugh no matter what he does. So he was very unhappy, very ill at ease as he started to sing an aria from opera. But when the beautiful strong virile tenor voice rang out my father's enthusiasm could be felt, and it was contagious. We all ended up in a riot as Jorge let out the last note.

My mother asked for a favorite song of hers, and Jorge sang it. Then he sang a lively Spanish song, and we all began to stamp our feet and clap our hands in rhythm. The excitement rose.

Then something unexpected happened. Mamacita jumped up, walked to the piano, and stood beside Jorge. She turned to Luis. "Play 'Júrame,' " she said. And she and Jorge sang it together.

Beside his ringing tenor her warm deep throbbing contralto sounded as true, as strong. Jorge took fire from her emotion. Luis played as never before. When they finished, we had a scene in our little *sala* like the ovations they used to give Calvé and Caruso. Everybody kissed and everybody cried. It was wonderful.

I learned that Mamacita had been studying opera when Papacito met her in Mexico City. Despite her teacher's pleas, for she wanted to give the world another Angela Peralta, Mamacita left her music and dedicated her life to giving the young engineer Porfirio Treviño Arreola a series of sons, and one daughter. No wonder she took so much interest in Jorge's singing, and thought so little of his forays into the movies.

When my parents bade me goodbye the next morning, before beginning their journey home, they said, "Well, darling, it has been like a visit to another world."

And my father added, "You will never return entirely to the twentieth century again."

As usual, he saw through to the essentials. I never will.

XXII

O N MANY LONG lazy Sundays at the *ranchito*, I followed Papacito about and learned the story of his childhood. He was a slight man, silver haired, with hazel eyes, nervous and quick in all his movements, restlessly active, intensely affectionate. He had two passions: study, and his family. To the first he gave the daily gift of his mind. To the second he gave, daily, all the rest of himself.

His father, Don Cayetano Treviño, had been a federal judge when Lerdo lost power and the regime of Porfirio Diaz began. Diaz could not afford to have Lerdo men in important posts in his government, but he did not strip them of their honors. He simply transferred Don Cayetano to a remote outpost and ordered him to set up court there. This was Ensenada, Lower California, at that time months of weary travel away from Mexico City. The new post was virtually an exile.

I listened with bated breath to Papacito's memories of the strange trip overland by mule pack to Acapulco, the terrible trip up the coast in a Portuguese coastal steamer, their being put off at Cape San Lucas, and having to wait there and make signal fires in order to get passage on another ship up to San Diego, and the first awful weeks when they had to live under a spreading live-oak tree, for there were only rough barracks for a few soldiers.

Papacito was a blond child, and he was called "El Güero," or "The Fair One."

In Ensenada, at a little school started there, he met the boy who became the dearest friend of his youth. His name was David (it is written the same in Spanish, but pronounced Da-veed), but El Güero at once named him "Coyote." The two became inseparable. They hunted and trapped and fished together; they shared all their boyish dreams and plans.

"I could never tell you all our adventures," said Papacito, thinking of that far-off time, and that far-off place. "They were so wonderful, and so many!

"Then my father was transferred to another court, and I was sent to school in San Diego," Papacito recalled. "I had to say goodbye to Coyote. As boys will do, we made a vow, and signed it in our blood (I don't know why we didn't get blood poison, pricking our arms with our rusty pocket knives) that we would always write to each other, at least once a month, as long as we lived! The exaggerated vows of children.

"But Eleesabet, we have kept our vows! Both David and I. He still lives in Ensenada, and I have not seen him for sixty years. But we have written each month. I have pictures of his wife and his children. He has pictures of mine."

And a few days after this conversation Mamacita rang me up in great excitement.

"Eleesabet! What do you think? There was a letter for Porfirio from his old friend David, the one he called 'Coyote.' "

"How nice. What did it say?"

"It was to say that Don David is coming to Monterrey. He is driving here with his wife and daughter, on the way to Mexico City. They will stay with us for a few days. Papacito is beside himself! We will have a big dinner to welcome them. I will make *cocada*, and you must make me one of those fruit cakes from your grandmama's recipe."

"Of course, Mamacita!"

Then ensued such a hysterical baking, grinding, decorating, freezing, and tasting of sauces at Bolivar 492, as I have never seen before or since. Papacito wandered around in a dream, and started when people spoke to him. Mamacita made all the cooks cry and even Tia Rosa got rattled and made a gypsy's arm that wouldn't roll up, to her complete consternation.

The day when Don David was expected to arrive dawned bright and silken. He and his family were to start from Laredo at nine. Papacito was on the highway, at the entrance to Monterrey, at eleven. I had been pressed into service by Mamacita to arrange the flowers for the table, but when I had them done, they weren't good enough for Don David, and she took them all out of the vases and did them over again herself. The maids had everything under control at last in the kitchen, and were nervously giggling. Just before eleven Luis came for me, and we went to join Papacito where he waited for the visitors.

At the appointed place Papacito stood in the road hatless, peering toward the north. Cars whizzed by. Trucks bumbled past. 11:10. 11:20. At a quarter to twelve a black sedan drew to a stop along the highway about fifty yards distant. A stout little man with grizzled gray hair stepped out and started to run toward Papacito, arms outstretched. Papacito gave a great shout. "Coyote!" "Güero!" They embraced. And then they stood there crying, and patting each other.

We met Don David's wife, a tall beautiful dark-eyed lady, with hair only faintly tinged with silver, and his lovely daughter of seventeen, who looked like a doe-eyed Bambi in human form. Then Papacito got in Don David's car. Papacito's chauffeur took his car into the city ahead, to show the way. We brought up the rear. When we arrived all the rest of the family had been assembled and were present.

We were all introduced, and the ladies were taken into Mamacita's bedroom to freshen up while Papacito and Don David huddled together in the office, talking a mile a minute. "Do you remember?" we heard a thousand times that day, before the wonderful banquet Mamacita served, during it, and afterwards, all afternoon, at the Banco de las Flores. Nobody else could get their attention. The two old gentlemen relived their childhood in every loved detail.

When Don David and his family continued on their journey, Papacito was comforted by the plans they had made. They would drive back through Monterrey and would stay a week, on their homeward journey. Papacito and Don David would camp at the *ranchito* and do everything they used to do together when they were boys. They would set traps and go hunting and fish. The car had not disappeared down the highway toward Mexico City before Mamacita was scheming what sort of wonderful menu she would make for them on their return.

But alas, Don David's wife became ill in Mexico City, grew worse. Within a week she was dead. Don David sold his car and took her body home to Baja California by rail. Papacito never saw Coyote again.

For that very winter, dear Papacito, too, left us forever.

XXIII

ARLY ONE WINTER morning I was in the kitchen making breakfast when I heard the phone ring in the front of the house. Luis went to answer it. Pale and shaken, he came back to tell me that Papacito was dead. As soon as he could dress, he went at once to Bolivar Street. I was told to wait until I was sent for.

Papacito had had several attacks of severe pain. Lately he had admitted this to me. After a movie one evening, he sent Mamacita home in the car but wanted to walk himself. The pain seized him suddenly. But by this time he was near the little Plaza of San Luis Gonzaga, and he staggered to a bench to wait out the attack. Somehow he got home afterward and fell into bed.

"But Papacito, you must take care of yourself," I had protested, frightened.

He shrugged his shoulders. "When the machine wears out, it has to be discarded. It does no good to wrap it up in cloths. What doesn't work is no good. And besides, you know, I can not stand idleness."

On this morning, I learned, he had risen early as he usually did, and had begun the day with one of his special pleasures, checking through a textbook of mathematics. When he found errors (as he often did), he wrote to the

author or the publisher, and thus established correspon-
dence that pleased him mightily.

Apparently he had found a very big mistake in one of
the problems he had been proving, and had begun a letter
about it. "And as a final point," he had written, and there,
pen in hand, he had dropped forward on the book. When
they lifted him, he was gone.

It was my good fortune that Papacito was fond of me.
He had come often to my house, unannounced, with his
violin, to play a few duets with me, or to sit and chat about
his childhood, and the turbulent panorama of his life.

As a little boy in Ensenada, having lived so freely in the
countryside, trapping and fishing, and learning the lore of
the wilds, he had fallen in love with the outdoors, and with
a life unhampered by routine. So when, some years later, he
was made to go to school, it seemed to him a horrible life.
At one point he went to his father, the judge, and firmly
asked to be allowed to stop and to go to work on a farm.

Don Cayetano, his father, very wisely arranged for him
to do so, and even selected the farm. He sent private
instructions, however, to the farm owner, to work the boy
hard from dawn until dusk and to let him know the
moment the youngster had had enough. So the farmer
woke El Güero in the darkness and told him to hitch up
and start to plow. About ten, and small for his age, the
plucky lad couldn't reach up to harness the big work
animals, nor were there any fences or benches to climb up
on. But El Güero found a shovel and with this he dug a
deepish pit, about six feet long, and into it he marched the
horse, and then harnessed him.

He stood the work, he became useful at it, but rebellion
simmered again when the farm owner wouldn't let him

read (instructions from Don Cayetano). El Güero had hated the confinement of a stuffy school room, when the whole world was full of sunshine and sweet air, but a life without books proved unbearable too.

He thought things over soberly and finally went home to ask to be returned to school. After that he never stopped studying. He chose engineering as a career, because it seemed to combine the outdoor life with the studies he liked best.

Papacito was in sympathy with the Revolution in many ways, but conditions became worse rapidly and he soon found that he would have to leave Mexico, as many others were doing, if he expected to be able to feed his ten children. Then chance gave him a way to escape.

One day he came home to find Mamacita pallid; a friend had come to advise her that the Carranzistas were about to take the city, and they intended to name Papacito Chief of the Northern Mexican Railway. (Because there were by that time so few engineers left that they could name to any post!) However, if Papacito accepted such a post, his head would be forfeit when the Villistas surged into Monterrey once more. And they were always near by.

But Papacito was undaunted; he accepted the post. Then he said he wanted to inspect the line as far as Laredo and ordered a private car ostensibly for that purpose. Next he got his family and all the friends he could manage into it, inspected the line to Laredo, and then hurried across the border to the United States.

But he did not have as sad a time in the United States as many distinguished and learned Mexicans did, who because they knew no English, had to become taxi drivers, or night watchmen. Papacito knew English well, and after he had won several contests for city sewage and drainage plans (in Victoria, Texas, and in some eastern cities), he began to work with an American firm of engineers. By then the Tampico oil boom was on and he was offered a position there at an astronomical salary. He and Mamacita were now very homesick for Mexico, so he took the job.

But the astronomical salaries were balanced by astronomical costs of living. Eventually Papacito found what he wanted and settled into a life of activity as City Engineer for Monterrey, and Professor of Mathematics at the University of Nuevo Leon. And there were wonderful nights over Monterrey when, on a rooftop with his cronies and a good telescope, he could study the stars as they revolved overhead.

Now at last he lay dead with his head on a textbook of mathematics.

Perhaps because of his reverence for science and his interest in proof of facts, Papacito was a free thinker.

"I was married in the church, Eleesabet," he told me, "and I will go to church once more. When they bury me."

So it was. But Mamacita, lovingly pious and always unhappy about his lack of orthodox religion, put her own rosary into his hands as he lay in his coffin, and from then until her own death, she devoted herself to prayers and masses for his soul.

Luis came to tell me that he would not obligate me to use the prescribed mourning. "You are an American," he said. "You will not be expected to do these things."

"But I want to do as the family does."

He looked at me with uncertainty.

"You don't know what you are saying."

"I can learn."

I did not want Luis to be put to the pain of explaining

why I did not follow the customs, accepting tacit criticism of me, making excuses for me. I asked Mamacita what were the rules, and I followed them in all except one particular. I did not close my piano and stop all music in my home. But I moved it to the back of the house, and played very softly. Nobody need think the lie that I had not loved Papacito, too.

Mourning is a complicated business in Mexico, especially in the provinces, to this day.

First the clothes. I learned that it was not enough to dress in black. I had to be very careful about what materials were used in my black dress. Taffeta was too chic. Satin was too luxurious. A dull crepe was best. Stockings could not be sheer or a flesh color. A dark lisle was best, or heavy black silk. Collars should be high, and sleeves long. No hat, but on the hair a special mourning veil made of a dull-black gauze. Not even the black lace mass veil was permitted to members of a house in mourning. This veil, after a month, might be attached to a small cloche hat. Or it could be worn indefinitely, pinned on, or tied on with cords. Little girls tie the cords under their chins.

Men also wear black suits, shoes, hats and ties, during the mourning period, and for some time after, a black band on the lapel or the sleeve. The black tie is so evident of mourning, that many men never wear any other color neckware after the death of someone very dear to them . . . mother, wife, or favorite child.

The widow customarily wears unrelieved black for three years. She may then use a touch of white. After five years she may dress in discreet dark colors.

The mourning period for one's mother is two years, for one's father, a year, for a brother or a child, a year. Other relatives according to the affection one feels. Widows very often simply go into black forever and ever, amen. Families are large in Mexico, and this means that mourning periods frequently overlap. That is why one sees Mexican women so very often dressed in black. And that is why, perhaps, my husband hates me to wear black, and insists that I use some brilliantly colored scarf or accessory, whenever I select a smart black suit or the "little black basic" dress. Black has been too basic in Mexico, and it induces a conditioned reflex in him.

In Monterrey, especially in the poorer districts, a reflection on the hard lot of children in a country which for years had a very high rate of infant mortality, is the fact that the death of a child is treated almost like a joyous occasion, by all except the bereaved parents themselves. The child is now a little angel, and will not suffer more in this vale of tears.

My maid Hilaria was devoted to *angelitos* and frequently arrived late to work because she had stopped in to visit one. Dead children were still laid out in the windows of their homes (when I first went to Monterrey to live), dressed as angels, and anyone might come in and stand for a few moments in the presence of a celestial being. The children of the poor were usually dressed in white or a color, wore little gold paper crowns, and sometimes golden wings. Surely some scent of Paradise must cling round the little earthly figure of the child who was at this moment by the side of Our Lord, in Heaven.

So strong is the feeling that children taken by death are that day in Heaven, that the black-bordered death announcements left at homes of friends, and printed in the newspapers, run something like this:

THE CHILD
MARIA DE LAS MERCEDES SANTOS DAVILA
FLEW UP TO HEAVEN
TODAY AT 3:30.
HER AFFLICTED PARENTS, GRANDPARENTS,
BROTHERS AND SISTERS, AUNTS AND UNCLES,
COMMUNICATE THE SAD NEWS.
MONTERREY, N.L.

I had to be careful to remember the rules of mourning, for they were many.

Besides the clothes, all pictures of mundane subjects were to be turned to the wall, or covered with black drapes. One prays the Rosary in the bereaved household for nine consecutive days, and all members of the family confess and receive communion on the days when memorial masses are held. These are held each month on the day of the death, and then, afterward, every year, on the date of the death.

Persons in deep mourning are not supposed to go to mass at the fashionable hours of twelve or one, but very early in the morning, preferably before it is yet light.

They do not go out to any sort of diversion, nor accept any engagements of any kind except to family reunions of a very solemn or intimate kind.

Before I married Luis I had harbored the point of view that the mourning family should be distracted. I thought we should help each other forget our sorrow and go about our duties made braver by some gentle diversion such as music or a ride through the countryside. I thought the family must be helped not to give in to their despondency, and encouraged not to brood over what cannot be changed.

But in Mexico I learned that my point of view was

considered perfectly heartless. One did not lament over the person whose grief wore him to a shadow; one admired him. One did not admire fortitude in the presence of death; one admired abject grief. One admired complete surrender, complete obedience.

The difference lies in the fact the Americans and Mexicans do not venerate the same quality of character in connection with the fact of death. Americans, I think, admire courage. One hears "She is so brave," murmured about mothers or wives who bear their loss in silence and go on about their regular duties.

But in Mexico sorrow is not considered heartbreaking, pitiful, or disfiguring. It is considered to be a mark of God's favor, by which one is ennobled and purified.

The attitude toward pain partakes of Papacito's own stoicism to it (for he knew he had angina pectoris and would die soon), and of the feeling that pain, too, must be borne as a mark of God's love, since only through pain may we share any part of His passion.

The man or woman wracked with pain or borne down by sorrow, stands close to the Man of Sorrows, and spiritually at least, is to be envied by those of us who are safe and soft in our comfort and happiness.

I cannot pretend that I learned this attitude at once. And it was years after I had come to understand it, that I took it for my own. Indeed, the first altercation I had with Mamacita was on the same subject. I had cried wildly that I would never suffer some dreadful incurable disease, that I would kill myself first. But she turned on me with great severity and said in words I have never forgotten, "No, Eleesabet. You will accept your debts to life when and as God sends them, and you will pay them every one."

One of our dearest friends was a wealthy, lively, and cultured lawyer, Don Eleazar. He had enjoyed a wonderful life. He had traveled the world over. He knew every niche and corner of his own Mexico, and he was at home in the great cities of Europe and the United States. He frequently took as many as ten or twelve relatives with him on long tours abroad. He entertained lavishly and set his table with delicate foods and fine wines.

When he was in his early sixties, he had a series of digestive upsets. He grew worse. An exploratory operation was recommended. It was learned that he had inoperable cancer of the liver.

He had been a devoted Catholic all his life, a member of the lay order of the Franciscans. Now his faith became all his life to him. He ordered his wife and relatives and doctors to give him no opiates, nor in any way to dull his senses or kill his consciousness.

"God has been good to me, lavish with his gifts. Now He awards me the greatest gift of all. I am to be permitted to share, in small measure, His pain. I who have adored him in every way I know, am to be allowed to approach him. It is as if I were offered the glory of the stigmata. Blessed be God."

And so it was.

I recount this because I feel that no amount of study of the Indian races, careful cataloging of handicrafts and music, and research into the language and history of Mexico, can give a true picture of the soul of the Mexican people, until a man like Don Eleazar is understood in his deeply proud and valiant mysticism. This type of character was sent Mexico by Spain, and is part of the country still, in every stoical and spiritual Mexican. And there are millions of them, who against this measure of their faith, gauge every action of their lives, and weigh every custom, tradition and activity.

When I went into mourning for Papacito, I found the first days taken up with my sorrow, with attendance at Rosary and Mass, with trying to comfort my husband and his family. But later, as the days went by so slowly, and I was not permitted to leave the house, nor receive more than a few quiet visitors, I found myself terribly restless and distraught. I went through a month of positively painful boredom, until I had to learn to return to the contemplative and tranquil arts I had been taught in my childhood. It took some severe adjustment, but after six months in thoughtful silence with my embroidery, my plants, my books of history, I had reached the other extreme of the pendulum. When I took off my black and began to wear white (in the hot summer months) and again ventured into the little world of Monterrey, it was with a sigh of sorrow.

I mourned for Papacito and to this day I miss him and often wish him near, so that we could discuss some of the things which perplex me. But also I miss those golden hours in my little patio, with only Poli for company, when I sat and matched colors and stitched at my embroidery, as the sun sank, re-examining all the ideas I had thought of as a permanent part of my equipment, for so many years. On close scrutiny I found I had to reject some. But others held their ground firmly. Slowly, but for always, I learned the great lesson—that in acceptance there is a special happiness.

XXIV

W HEN I CAME to live in Mexico I had no idea
that I was going to become so intimately involved
with the saints. I had always known that there were saints.
I longed passionately for Joan of Domremy to be canon-
ized; I realized that a lot of my future happiness would
depend on St. Peter. But I didn't know that the saints,
hosts of them, were going to be in and out of my life like
neighbors. Some of them came to be as close as friends
who phoned me daily; others were powerful, to be turned
to in time of tribulation, as one remembers the rich relative when broke; some became trusted confidants, who
never let me down. Others I loved through thick and thin,
though often they were capricious and childish with me,
refusing me the simplest favors.

When my birthday arrived, that first year after I was
married, I arose planning on a cake and fried chicken. I
looked forward to presents and boxes of candy and bunches
of flowers. But Luis was preoccupied through breakfast,
chatty but conspicuously unfestive at lunch, and at dinner
he complained at the toughness of the chicken.

"It's my birthday," I announced, darkly.

"That so?" He resumed his struggle with the chicken.

Suddenly a thought struck him and he looked up at me worriedly.

"You haven't been phoning people, telling them how old you are, I hope?"

This was too much. I left the table in floods of disappointed tears. Luis came after me, dried my eyes, and told me to put my coat on, we were going to Mamacita's.

"To choose a saint for you," he told me.

Mamacita explained to me that birthdays were nothing in Mexico. Only children had them, adults just ignored them.

"We celebrate our saint's day," she explained. "Luis celebrates the 21st of June, the day of San Luis de Gonzaga, not the fifth of August, when he was born. My day is December sixteenth, the day of Santa Adela. Now you are Eleesabet. There are many saints named Eleesabet, or Isabel, as we say in Spanish. There was the aunt of the Holy Virgin, who was old and barren, until the Lord put life into her womb, after she had lost all hope."

"I suppose you think the barren old lady would be a good saint for me," I muttered unhappily, for it had been made clear to me that hags rising thirty should conceal their years like revolting deformities.

Mamacita hastened to turn up another Saint Eleesabet.

"There was the Queen of Hungary," she offered me. "She took loaves to the poor, and was greatly beloved. But her day is celebrated on November nineteenth, and I can tell you from experience that it is inconvenient to have a saint's day so near Christmas. People are likely to think that one present would do for both dates."

"Still, she sounds nice," I admitted.

Warming up to the subject, Mamacita went on, "She

was so charitable and kind that she took home a leper and nursed him in her own bed."

"Oh dear!" This morsel about the leper chilled me, for though it aroused my admiration, it was quite clear to me that I could never rise to follow the example of the Queen of Hungary, so it seemed presumptuous to name her my saint. I just knew I wasn't going to be able to put a leper in my bed.

"Well," said Mamacita briskly, "why should we bother with such foreign saints anyhow, Central Europeans and Slavs, when we have a perfectly good Latin like ourselves, Santa Isabel of Portugal? Her day falls on July eighth, a very nice date, and besides, she was a Spaniard by birth! She was Isabel of Aragon, Queen of Portugal."

I plumped for the Queen of Portugal.

But I soon learned that I was going to have dealings with many other saints as well.

I took up with San Antonio de Padua in a hasty, opportunistic way, I confess, though he never held it against me. It is a relationship that has deepened with the years. I ring him up, via urgent ejaculations and sudden prayers, several times a day, and I believe I may say that we are devoted friends. Many are the miracles he has made for me, as proof of his power and his kindness.

We met in the following manner. I had been home to visit my mother in California, and had taken a bus to Los Angeles, where I was to board the train for Mexico. But on arrival in Los Angeles, I learned that the bus company had lost my luggage somewhere en route. I waited for it for two days, and then I had to finish my journey. Nothing more was heard of the luggage for several months, and then at last I got a communication from the bus company saying that they had traced it everywhere possible, they had no idea what had become of it, and they were willing to pay me a hundred dollars indemnity for it. Now I had jewelry, presents, and other treasures in the suitcase, besides my clothes, and one hundred dollars would not have been adequate compensation. I was distracted.

But when I told this sad tale to a friend she said to me, "Have you tried San Antonio? He is the patron of lost objects."

"No. Tell me what to do," I implored.

"You must make an exercise in humility, and do an act of contrition for your sins, and say a novena, that is a prayer on nine consecutive days. Then, if there is no reason why you should not have your luggage back, San Antonio will give it to you."

"How do I do the exercise?"

"San Antonio's day is the thirteenth of the month and falls on a Tuesday. From each of thirteen strangers, you must ask a penny, saying it is for an offering to San Antonio. This is an exercise in humility, to cleanse you of pride. You must take these pennies and begin your prayers on a Tuesday, and if there is no fateful reason why you shouldn't have back your things, you will get them."

I faithfully performed the rites, and I am here to remark that accosting the thirteen strangers to ask for a penny did a lot to give me an idea of my proper station in life. I said the prayers. Nothing happened. I was ready to backslide disastrously. But when I got home, I found a letter from my mother. In it, she said, "An odd thing happened. A few minutes ago the bus company drove up and delivered your lost suitcase. I checked right away, and everything is in it. It had been to Alaska and back. To make certain, I myself will bring it to you."

Thus San Antonio, bless and love him, got me back my suitcase, and brought my mother for a visit as well.

And many are the lost objects he has found for me, from my passport to a silver thimble. In fact he so overwhelms me with his favors that I am ashamed, and will not often ask for myself, but every time I ask, with a full heart, for something for anyone I love, San Antonio's generosity is immediately forthcoming.

Mexican girls believe that if they beg him, he will get them a sweetheart. A friend of mine recounted to me that this was indeed so. She had bought herself a small image of San Antonio, and made one novena after the other to him, asking for a good, kind and faithful man to become her *novio* and later her husband.

"And what happened?"

"Well, I said five separate novenas and nothing happened, and I had an access of rage, and took the image and threw it out of the window!"

"Oh, you horrible girl!"

"And San Antonio fell on the head of a young man walking by in the street and knocked him cold. They brought him into our *sala* here for first aid. We're to be married in March."

Direct action.

San Antonio will get you a sweetheart, but he has a stern Catholic attitude toward love and marriage. No frivolity, no foolishness. Once he gets you the sweetheart, you can never change your mind. The saint's gifts are not exchangeable.

What redress is there then? For everybody knows that even in Catholic countries, not all husbands are everything they should be. Well, there is an out. There is San Benito. San Benito is always depicted in the garb of one of the monastic orders, his arms outspread in compassion. I was startled to see that those arms were so often draped thickly with lengths of ribbon in various colors, and one day I plucked up courage to ask why.

"Oh," said my friend Margarita, "those show that somebody has been measured."

"Measured? But why?"

"Well, suppose your husband has been perfectly horrible to you, has beaten you, and shamed you in public, or pawned your jewelry, or something. You measure him, and lay his measure over the arm of San Benito, and say a prayer."

"What is the prayer?"

"It goes like this. 'Dear San Benito, here is his measure. Straighten him out, or carry him away.' "

"Meaning . . . ?"

"Carry him away. You know. To Purgatory, or . . . wherever."

"Oh."

San Benito being in the back of my mind at all times, like an ace in the hole, I constantly studied his image in the churches I visited. But no matter where I went, I always found him weighed down with ribbons, frightfully busy, booked solid for months ahead.

In Mexico all the saints are thus delegated certain down-to-earth, practical duties. For guidance in the choice of a profession, you turn to San Rafael. San Jorge will protect you from dragons and other mythical beasts, should any get loose, but he will also take care of scorpions and centipedes. San Isidro will see that you and your family are never without bread. San Anselmo will sweeten up a nagging wife. Saint Gertrude will help if your cat gets the yellow vomit.

I learned that Santa Maria Magdalena is the protectress of repentant women, but also she is patroness of the perfumers. This has never ceased to seem sinister to me, but perhaps that is because a year of college French taught me the general meaning of the names of perfumes.

Besides the saints for every day in the year, there are saints who will protect you against danger (Santa Genoveva against the fever, Santa Barbara against lightning, Santa Balbina against fires), and so on.

But the really sensible thing to do is to pick out a powerful patron saint and stay with her or him through everything. You get to be like relatives, and the saint probably says to herself, "Oh, that tiresome girl, she's in a jam again. But I'll have to get her out. After all, she's mine." Like an aunt.

Mamacita was devoted with all her heart to the Virgin of Lourdes, who appeared in the manifestation of Our Lady of the Immaculate Conception. Luis loves Our Lady of Carmel beyond all others, as do my friend Margarita, and Josefina. Clementina, Doña Leonor, and Maria are faithful children of Our Lady of Guadalupe. Tio Jorge is fondest of Saint Peter. Luisa Maria finishes one novena to Santa Eduviges (Hedwig) only to begin another. Patricia and Estela are never without their blessed image of the Lady of the Sacred Heart; she is patroness of hopeless and despaired-of causes. Alma and Isabel render daily homage to San Judas.

How can one say why one chooses one saint above all others? It is a form of love, as inexplicable as is the nature of love. I only know that just as Mamacita's heart turned in all fullness to Our Lady of Lourdes, so mine turns to Our Lady of the Rosary, especially in her appearance to the little shepherds of Fatima, and to San Antonio. Though I have been steadily drawn to Our Lady of the Sorrows, and when I walk in her procession, as I have done on Good Friday, I, who have been so extraordinarily fortunate in my life, can perceive the abyss of knowing all the world's sorrow, as She does.

The Procession of Our Lady of the Sorrows is a strange and deeply emotional one. In Mexico it is called "The Encounter." I did not know about this ancient Spanish ceremony until I was invited to take part in it. I was told to come to the church in a black dress, with a black mantilla or veil, and wearing my veil over a high-backed Spanish comb, if I had one. As darkness fell, the procession formed. Our Lady of the Sorrows was carried on the shoulders of black-garbed men, while in front walked the vested priest and the acolytes, swinging censers.

Behind the image, two by two, walk the oldest ladies of the parish, then the other married women, and last the unmarried girls, and men and boys. Each person in the procession carries a tall lighted taper, and the parade winds through the church gardens in absolute silence. Into the street we went, in perfect silence, nothing but the whisper of the women's skirts, the creak of the censer, the soft placing of shoes on the path.

As we turned to go back to the church, another silent procession emerged, carrying the image of Our Lord Crucified. In silence, by the flickering candlelight, the images met. The Encounter. In silence, everyone stands perfectly still, and with a shock of recognition, one feels in her own heart, the seven swords of sorrow, which pierced the heart of Mary.

But though the Spanish rites can call up storms of suffering, they can be lively and childlike, with a lovely sense of joy. As on Christmas Eve, when the church doors swing back to admit the prettiest young girl of the parish, in a wide-skirted dress of coral silk, her hair covered with a white lace Spanish mantilla, bearing in her arms the image of the Infant Jesus. To the music of castanets and tambourines, she walks down the main altar, to give the Holy Child into the arms of the waiting priest, who then lays Him in the manger. This young girl, the god-mother of the Holy Infant, may hear mass at a *prie-dieu* inside the altar rail, but when she rises to leave the church after mass, again the lively, young music sounds, and one feels all the joy of youth at seventeen as she passes.

As the days went by, it came over me that in Mexico one lives not by the calendar year, but by the liturgical year. One's life, the feasts that mark the milestones passed in time's progress, are part of the turning of the year from Advent and Nativity to Lent and the Passion and Pentecost. Sparkling through the months are the jewel colors of the days that help us relive, in devotion and memory, the life of the Christ. Ruby of Christmas, amethyst of penitential Lent, the dazzling radiance of the diamond that is Resurrection, the glowing emerald green (for hope) which is Pentecost.

By the time my saint's day arrived, I had learned all the ritual.

At dawn, I heard the *mañanitas*, which are a morning

serenade, always sung on one's saint's day. My family had gathered outside the barred windows of my little house, and woke me with the ancient song.

> "These are the morning songs
> That we sang for King David,
> But as today is your saint's day,
> Dear, we sing them for you!"

There are many verses, but one hears only enough to give one time to dress, and then rush out, and let the singers in, and exchange kisses and *abrazos*, and lead everyone to a big Mexican breakfast of "*ranchero* eggs" (done in a hot chile sauce), and fried beans and tamales and *pulque* bread and chocolate and coffee with hot milk.

Breakfast lasts as long as anyone will sit and tell anecdotes and have a drop more chocolate. Say until eleven in the morning. Then there are gifts in the *sala* . . . the potted flower you admired, the perfume you longed for, the set of oven dishes, the new gloves.

On that first saint's day of mine, Mamacita gave me my black lace mass veil, the traditional Spanish mantilla, which is worn over a high comb in Spain, but softly draped over the dressed hair, in Mexico.

And from that day forward, at Mass, or after dark, or visiting friends who were in mourning, I was as all the other ladies of the city, a discreet figure in black, my hair covered by the mantilla of black lace, the black jet cross of Dolores at my throat.

XXV

AN AMERICAN FRIEND visited me, and tried to share for a time the life that has become mine.

"When do we take off our masks, put on our hats, and walk off the stage?" she demanded. It seemed incredible to her that I had become part of the pattern of a life so alien to her.

"Didn't you have to make terrific adjustments?" she asked.

"I suppose I did," I answered humbly, "but I can't remember when I did, or how."

Once when the phone rang, and I answered, she listened open-mouthed.

"*Bueno?*" I asked, as is customary, and when the voice wanted to know, in Spanish, who was speaking, I answered, of course, "Eleesabet."

My friend said, "Well, that does it. You don't even know your own name any more."

"*Sea por Dios,*" I answered, which is good Mexican custom too, and means, "As God wills," or "Maybe so."

"I've figured it out," she said, after thought. "You have two ventricles and two auricles, and they don't know which kind of blood they are pumping around, Mexican or American."

And what could I say to that?
Another good Mexican phrase, when in doubt.
"*Pues, quien sabe?*"

Epilogue to the 1971 Edition

I

T IS NOW almost forty years since the events in this chronicle took place, and almost twenty since they were written and published. In taking a backward look at those years, I am overcome by the changes that have occurred in the world, in Mexico, in my life.

The atomic bomb has become a reality, offering us, like God Himself, eternal damnation or the chance to make a heaven on earth. We now get instant news via satellite, and men walk on the moon.

Being so near the United States, Mexico feels all the great winds of change that blow through our country, from rapid industrialization and mobility via four-lane highways and enormous jets, to the unrest of youth, the convulsions within the Roman Catholic church, and the crisis in education.

Mexico is now in the forefront of the Latin American republics, with her fifth successive civilian President. The greatest part of the national budget goes for education. A system of social security has been implanted and is being extended to all classes as rapidly as possible. Technological schools train young Mexicans in all the academic and applied sciences. Air conditioning is a commonplace. Ladies watch television comedies which are supported by ads for detergents. The hum of the washing machine is heard in the land, and Mexico makes her own cornflakes, packaged hotcake flour, and instant coffee. The bullfight is yielding to soccer and baseball; young men wear long, flowing locks and beards, and girls are seen on city streets in every variety of trousers.

Mexico is in the mainstream.

Yet, when recently I ruffled through the pages of *My Heart Lies South,* I found, to my great delight, that in one respect the book is not even slightly dated. It was written to reveal to Americans what went on behind the barred windows and the big *zaguáns,* and it told about the Mexican family. This has not changed.

Mexican devotion to a strong, united family is still the outstanding characteristic of the mores in cities as well as in the provincial towns and the country.

In the cities, young girls may go to work in shops and in offices—a few study professions—but they live at home. And they stop working when they marry.

Mamacita used to say, "Eleesabet, two things keep the family together—the church bell and the dinner bell." The observation is still valid. Children obey their parents. Young people marry in church and christen their babies. They continue to visit and to love and respect their elders. There are no more old folks' homes, in proportion to the populace, than there were fifty years ago, and they were almost unknown then. Orphanages, too, are scarce. Families take care of their own.

Typical is a remark made to me at a tea party when I said that I would soon undertake a long trip to visit my mother. "Ay," cried a friend, "if I still had my Mamacita on this earth, I would go to the end of the world to be with her."

Mamacitas—some like my husband's mother, who was valiant, merry, and wise; others more solemnly tender and dutiful; but all adored, protected, and important—run what is still basic in Mexico: the family.

Herein lies, I believe, the strength of the country and the immense attraction of Mexican life for foreigners, especially for Americans. Visitors in Mexico who have an opportunity to savor the atmosphere of the Mexican home, feel for it not only affection but a deep nostalgia.

In the years since *My Heart Lies South* was published, I have received literally thousands of letters which have told me that Mamacita, my husband's enchanting mother, had become very dear to them. But not only Mamacita. One day in Mexico City I received a phone call from a lady who said, "You don't know me, but I know you, for I have read your book about your Mexican family. I wanted to tell you that I planned my trip to Mexico with a stopover in Monterrey so that I could go out to the cemetery and leave some flowers on Papacito's grave."

I treasure a letter that came from a young girl in Detroit, who told me that she and a number of her friends, all living alone in the city and working there, had formed a "Mamacita Club." They met whenever any one of them had a problem, and they would discuss it and try to figure out what advice Mamacita might have given.

My husband's family, at first somewhat taken aback at my invasion of their privacy, have long since taken me to their grateful hearts, because I made so many people acquainted with their beloved Mamacita and Papacito, and because my book was a tribute to them.

Because of the book, I have had considerable success as a marriage counselor. Mexican boys have brought me their American sweethearts, that I might convince them of the high worth of Mexican husbands. And American girls by the dozen have written and have come to see me, posing nervous questions about contemplated marriages to Mexicans. What about adjustments, achieving meaningful relationships, togetherness, and personal independence, they worried. All these things awaken serious thought in me, for I had never heard of any of them when, all starry-eyed, I married the first Mexican I met when I crossed the border.

My answer to all young couples is the same: You must love each other. If you marry across racial, religious, and cultural lines, you must love more and harder.

On a recent trip to Monterrey, I walked past our first home on Morelos Street. It is in a commercial section now, and there is a shop where our *sala* used to be. Nevertheless I learned (and I was deeply touched) that some drivers who take tourists through the town to show them the sights, point out our little house and announce, "And there is the house where lived Luis and Eleesabet."

Mamacita is long gone. After Papacito's death, she went through the motions of living like someone who is distracted because late for an appointment, so eager was she to join him.

Gone, too, are Tia Rosa and Tia Cuca, Jorge and Ernesto, Carlos, Oscar and Ricardo, dear Tocayo, and so many others we knew and loved in Monterrey forty years ago.

But beyond the shop and its counters, I can look back into memory and see my little *sala* as it was. Luis sits playing the piano, Policarpo purrs on the rug, my children totter about on baby legs; Papacito rushes through the house to check on the grandsons; Mamacita and Jorge stand by the piano, singing "Júrame." And I see myself, living so busily, making mistakes, learning by doing, as they say. I was then, as now, so safe, so happy, within that fortress — the Family.

Elizabeth Borton de Treviño
Cuernavaca, 1971

About the Author

BEST KNOWN for her 1966 Newbery Award winning book, *I, Juan de Pareja,* Elizabeth Borton de Treviño has written extensively as a journalist and as a novelist in a long and varied writing career. She was first published at the age of 8, when *The Monterey Peninsula Herald* printed one of her poems. It was many more years and many a page later before she saw her name consistently in print. In her university years, one teacher would read her tragic plays aloud to the class, making them shout with laughter and Miss Borton retire in tears. She would later consider this experience as one of her most valuable lessons. This same teacher told her, as she recounts in her Newbery Award acceptance speech, "You might just possibly," he said in his dry English way, "have the makings of a writer in you. For I couldn't make you stop writing, and essentially that is what writing boils down to. People who allow themselves to be discouraged are not for this trade."

Elizabeth Borton was born in 1904 in Bakersfield, California into a family bound to form and develop the trait of stubborn persistence that would carry her on to writing success. Her father was a lawyer who loved his vocation and had worked his way through law school by arising at 4 A.M. to deliver newspapers. When counseled to find a small town and grow with it, he picked Bakersfield, considered a "hardship post." After one day, his new bride suggested they start saving to move somewhere else, but they never left. Here Elizabeth and her sister and brother lived happily in a time when the predominant horse and carriage were being overtaken by the automobile, the steam engine and the trolley car. The author describes these years, and the subsequent ones, in *The Hearthstone of My Heart* (1977).

Originally traveling to Boston to study the violin, Elizabeth ended up as a journalist for *The Boston Herald* where her music background and her fluency in Spanish established her as an interviewer of international celebrities. It was on one of her assignments for the paper that she met her future husband. It was also around this time that she wrote the first of five *Pollyanna* stories. This writing was good practice, but Elizabeth needed all she'd ever learned about perseverance before she finally moved beyond this slight beginning. After another novel, which met with little success, her writing career became established in 1953 with the best selling *My Heart Lies South*.

Elizabeth Borton de Treviño wrote one other memoir, besides the two already mentioned, entitled *Where the Heart Is* (1962), telling of the years after those recounted in *My Heart Lies South*. *Carpet of Flowers* and *Nacar, the White Deer* are both children's stories about Mexico and reflect a growing identification with the faith she made her own upon marriage to Luis. *El Güero* (1989) is about Papacito's adventures as a young boy.

The author lived until her death in December, 2001 in her beloved adopted country of Mexico.